Undercover
with the
a Brotherhood of the Sword novel
Earl

Tami~

Undercover
with the
a Brotherhood of the Sword novel
Earl

ROBYN
DEHART

So great to meet you. Robyn DeHart

Entangled Publishing, LLC
2614 South Timberline Road
Suite 109
Fort Collins, CO 80525
Visit our website at www.entangledpublishing.com.

Scandalous is an imprint of Entangled Publishing, LLC.

Edited by Alethea Spiridon Hopson
Cover Design by Heidi Stryker & Liz Pelletier
Cover Art by The Killion Group, Inc.

ISBN 978-1-943892-05-1

Manufactured in the United States of America

First Edition August 2015

Scandalous
an Entangled imprint

To my brainstorming buds: Emily, Shane, Anne and Margo. Y'all are always available when I'm in a pinch and I so appreciate all the help and ideas!
Thanks to Alethea and Kevan, you make the business part of this writing gig a pleasure and I love working with both of you.
And to Paul, for everything.

Chapter One

It is a truth universally known that a girl entering her twenty-first year must be in want of a husband. But it was not a truth that Evelyn Marrington took to heart. She had no desire to marry now or any other time. Instead, she wanted to hole herself up in a sweet little cottage and write adventurous novels until her hair grayed and no one cared if she was a spinster.

Due to her family's financial straits and their middling social standing, Evie's chances of doing just that seemed rather good. However, her two older sisters had recently made very advantageous matches, thrusting their entire family into a more elevated social sphere. Flush with that success, Evie's mother was now determined to land an equally impressive husband for her middle daughter. Never mind that Evie's own wishes were modest and veered away from marriage. Her family obviously saw things quite differently, a fact she could not ignore with her mother pointing to every eligible man in the vicinity.

At the moment Evelyn longed to have a book in her hand. She could close her eyes and imagine the sound of the paper turning, the bold print of the words beckoning her into their adventure. Instead, she stood at the edge of the small ballroom doing her best to blend into the tapestry behind her while the rest of the guests of this house party danced merrily.

"Evelyn, dear, if you continue to sink yourself into the background, how are any of the men to see you and ask you to dance?" her mother said, placing a forceful hand on Evie's back, effectively shoving her forward.

"I do not care for dancing," Evelyn said, knowing full well that her protests would fall on deaf ears.

"Nonsense, what girl doesn't care to dance?"

There wasn't much that she and her mother agreed upon, except for the fact that they didn't agree on much. They were as different as the morning from the night, and though Evelyn did her best to refuse, her mother still worked her hardest to squeeze her middle daughter into the pretty package that was a perfect debutante. One might think that already achieving success with her first two daughters would have been enough to appease the Marrington matriarch, but she was not so easily pacified.

Evelyn sat precisely in the middle of the Marrington children. Portia and Jillian were her elder sisters and then came Catherine and Meghan. The two eldest Marrington girls were beautiful, lovely, poised, and had made a splash in Society. Portia was already married to the handsome and kind Viscount Handlebrook, and the Earl of Bellview had recently asked for Jillian's hand. This left Evelyn uncomfortably in the center of attention as the next Marrington daughter to find herself a good match.

If she had her sister's temperament, grace, and beauty, no doubt she would make such a match. Unfortunately, she was too quick-witted for simpering flirtations, too practical for ethereal grace, and, worst of all, her hair was an unpleasantly violent shade of red. In short, she did not currently have her sisters' options when it came to marriage.

In fact, her most promising suitor was the Viscount Edgerly, a portly widower sixteen years her senior. Not that she particularly minded the kindly Lord Edgerly, because, after all, beggars could not be choosers. It was his eleven children she minded. Based on his frantic desperation to find a wife, she suspected he was no more eager to parent them than she was.

While she was sure the Edgerly children were perfectly lovely, the fact that there were eleven of them meant marriage to the Viscount—no matter how advantageous in the eyes of her mother—was simply out of the question. She would have no time to write. Nay, she would have no time to breathe or eat or sleep. In short, she would do anything to escape that fate. Unfortunately, her other options were not much better.

"Didn't you dance with Sir Winters at the last Brighten soiree?" her mother asked. "I believe I see him across the room now."

Evelyn caught a glimpse of the man and winced. "And my toes are still bruised."

Portia smiled and linked her arm with Evelyn's. "Mama,

Evie is right. That poor man should not be allowed to dance, especially when he wears such heeled boots."

"He's quite obviously trying to mask the fact that he is shorter than a man ought to be," Jillian said.

Not to mention at least thirty years her senior, but Evelyn refrained from adding that. She slid behind her sisters so she would not be so easily visible to the older gentleman. He'd already been standing up on his toes, searching in their direction. He'd made it quite clear to her during their last dance that he was taken with her and interested in courting her. She'd come home from that ball and told her father, in no uncertain terms, that she was not available if the man came to call. Fortunately for her, her father did not seem too eager to marry her off to a man closer to his age than Evelyn's, and he'd artfully dismissed him when he'd paid a visit midweek.

Their mother laughed, but caught herself and placed her fan in front of her mouth. "Be that as it may, Sir Winters has a decent annual income and I don't believe our dear Evie can afford to be quite so selective when it comes to picking a suitor."

Because she wasn't as pretty as her older sisters. Or as gregarious. Her mother would never come out and say those things, but Evelyn felt certain that was what was missing.

"If you are smart, you will do what is necessary to trap that man into marriage this very weekend," her mother said.

"Honestly, Mother! I have no intentions of trapping any man into marriage," Evelyn said.

"Evie, you won't have to. You shall find the right man for you, just as Portia and I have," Jillian said.

She was so kind. She wasn't even trying to pander to

Evelyn, she actually believed that, believed that Evelyn would be able to find a love match just as her perfect, beautiful sisters had. But Evelyn knew the truth of her reality, and she had done her part to prevent from being put on the marriage mart. She'd begged her parents to not make her come out and they had agreed, but only partly. They did not have a ball to introduce her, but they had seen to it that she was properly introduced, and she obliged them by attending parties with the family and dancing at least once per evening.

It wasn't that she couldn't abide people, but rather couldn't stand to have people look at her, compare her to her sisters, or even her mother, who after five children was still quite the beauty. Evelyn looked more like her father's side of the family. She was short and because of that her body stubbornly held on to curves. So instead of her sisters who were delicate and graceful, she felt clumsy and stout.

Her two younger sisters ran over to them, all giggles and grins, whispering excitedly to their mother.

"What is it? Stop hissing in my ear. You know that drives me to distraction," Mother said, swatting at the air by her ear.

"Two new gentlemen have arrived," Meghan said breathlessly.

"They are drenched from the rain and stand dripping in the corridor," Catherine said.

Their mother clapped her hands once and leaned in. "Of course Evelyn shall have first choice among them."

It was more than enough for Evelyn to simply fade into the background and step away, but she knew her mother would find her. Two new gentlemen indeed.

"It is only Ellis," Jillian said from beside her, standing up on her toes. "Our dear cousin."

"Yes, but it does appear as if he has brought a friend," Portia said. "A very large and handsome friend."

Evelyn glanced out into the corridor and saw the man in question. He was tall, impossibly broad, and rain dripped from his fair hair and into his face.

"Isn't he dashing?" Catherine said dreamily.

"How could you possibly tell if he's handsome?" Evelyn asked before she thought better of it. "He's scowling."

Whispers scurried through the ballroom; the hushed words didn't take long to reach their ears, as the room was smaller than those public balls in London.

"'Tis Bennett Haile, the Earl of Somersby," the woman next to her mother said.

"An earl," her mother said eagerly. She looked over at Evelyn and smiled, that sort of secret, conspirator smile.

Another woman nodded approvingly. "I've heard he's some manner of a spy."

Two more women walked over to join the conversation. "All I've ever heard about him is that he jilted some poor girl, left her to marry a penniless viscount."

"Scandalous," the other whispered.

"Indeed, he's quite the rogue," the first woman stated.

"Good heavens, but he is a large man," her mother said.

"What is he doing here?" Jillian asked.

"It would seem that Ellis has brought him," her mother said.

"Whatever he's doing here, he seems to be staring directly at you, Evie," Portia said.

Evelyn glanced again at the stranger and he did, indeed, seem to be looking pointedly at her. Beneath the weight of his stare, she felt every bit the dowdy mess her mother had accused her of being earlier that day. Ellis said something to the hulking earl and the man gave a nearly imperceptible nod.

Her mother chortled delightfully. "Oh, it would seem that our dear cousin has finally answered my requests and brought Evelyn a suitor. And an earl, no less. Positively splendid."

Would that she could disappear into the floor, but Evelyn had never been that fortunate.

• • •

Bennett Haile, Earl of Somersby, looked around at the ballroom. Granted, it had been ages since he'd attended a ball in London, but he didn't recall them being quite so overrun with people. No matter what room he entered, he always towered over everyone around him, both in height and breadth. Here in this small ballroom in Essex, it was no different. Perhaps it was even more pronounced. It certainly didn't help matters that he and Ellis had gotten stuck in a rainstorm and were soaked.

The couples twirled gracefully on the ballroom floor; Beethoven's waltz accompanied their dance. He loathed dancing, had never been particularly skilled at it. He exhibited nothing but speed and precision when in the boxing prize ring, but in a ballroom, it did not translate. His feet were too big, his hands like a couple of hams, and his instincts muddled when so many bodies swirled about him.

Why was Potterfield meeting them here? Bennett had not quite so many questions when Ellis had requested he ride along with him to his cousins in Epping. But as they'd journeyed and he'd learned that Potterfield was to meet them, Bennett knew this was official Brotherhood business.

Bennett had been recruited into *Custos a Vesica,* the Brotherhood of the Sword, when he'd graduated from Oxford at the tender age of eighteen. He'd eagerly accepted the invitation to become a member of the elite security agency dedicated to protecting the monarch of England, expecting a life of danger and adventure. Over the last ten years there had been a good deal of that, and he was grateful he'd had an excuse to avoid society and the machinations of marriage-minded maidens. He was no more inclined to follow the rules and dictates of marriage than he was to follow the orders from his superiors to the letter. But he believed in the mission and the discipline required to fulfill it.

"Where is Potterfield?" Bennett asked Ellis. "Why the devil would he ask us to meet him here?"

Then as if the mere mention of his name summoned him, the man appeared. Sir Percival Potterfield entered, and obviously had travelled by coach as his person remained dry. Unlike Bennett and Ellis who still dripped on the rug. He was an unassuming man, shorter than most and thin with a balding head and nondescript features. Perhaps that was what made him so effective in his leadership of the Brotherhood. People weren't threatened by his humble appearance.

"Excellent, you both made it," Potterfield said as he came to stand beside them. He looked out into the ballroom and nodded. "Is that her?"

"Yes," Ellis said.

"I dare say, Ellis, the resemblance is quite remarkable," Potterfield said.

"Would either of you care to let me in on your little secret?" Bennett asked, keeping his voice low. "I'm beginning to worry you've brought me here to rusticate in your uncle's little village.

"Not at all, Somersby," Ellis retorted with a hint of a smile.

"Then what?" He had a sinking feeling as he followed his companion's gaze to the woman Potterfield had referred to. "Be so good as to tell me what the young lady has to do with anything."

Despite the fact that Ellis had pointed out the girl, Bennett had spotted her as soon as they'd entered the ballroom, as she stood out from the crowd. A wild poppy amidst a field of perfectly groomed roses. Her vibrant red hair, though tamed in a coiffure, fought against the constraints of the pins and several curls had sprung free, framing her fair face. There was no possible way for this woman to pose as Queen Victoria. Yes, there was some similarity in features, but while the Queen was a handsome woman, Miss Marrington was captivating. She was easily the comeliest of all the young ladies present, and Bennett could not fathom what Potterfield's interest in her was.

"Lady Fenwick!" Ellis said to the matron who approached them.

"My dear Lord Ellis. You are positively drenched!" the woman said. She managed to keep her distance from the puddles they were creating, and silently summoned servants to take away their sopping greatcoats.

"I apologize for intruding upon your good hospitality,"

Ellis said. "We should have stopped—"

"Nonsense! I have readied rooms for each of you," the lady said. "I am certain they will not be as grand as you are accustomed to, but I can assure you they are clean and well tended."

"That is very good of you, my lady," Potterfield said with a quick bow. "But a room for me won't be necessary as I am heading back to London tonight."

"In this weather? Are you certain? 'Tis no problem at all," the lady said.

"Pressing business, my lady, but I appreciate the hospitality."

Bennett barely heard the exchange. His clothes were dry enough now that his greatcoat was gone, but the young miss who'd garnered Potterfield's attention earlier held his gaze. She was so small and graceful, far too small for a colossus like him.

Bennett tore his eyes away from the flame-haired vixen. This whole night was becoming increasingly more curious, as well as uncomfortable. He could not figure what in blazes they were doing there.

He and the others followed a servant up the stairs and onto the third floor where they were shown to their bedchambers. All three men entered the room intended for Bennett and he surveyed the surroundings. Considering this was a smaller country estate to the one he was accustomed to, the accommodations were more than acceptable, from the large framed bed to the window seat. The rain still beat a rough staccato against the window.

He turned back to his companions. "What business is so urgent that we had to intrude upon a simple country ball?" Bennett asked as servants scurried out of the room. "I realize that we often have to be secretive about our meetings, but this seems a little extreme."

"I've called you here because of a concerning matter," Potterfield said after the servants had cleared. "As you know, Her Majesty was injured a few days ago at the opening of the Royal Ascot. Initially, we believed the injury was not serious, but it is apparent that it will take some time to heal."

Bennett withdrew from his waistcoat, then grabbed a linen cloth from the basin and began drying his face and hands. He found a thin black ribbon in his coat pocket and after wringing the towel through his wet hair, he pulled it back and tied it into a queue. "What happened, precisely, as I was not there?" he asked.

"Someone bumped into her and she fell. Her ankle is quite swollen and it will take some time to heal up so that she can walk normally. The physician doesn't seem to believe it is serious, merely an injury that will require her to be off her feet in order for her to heal," Potterfield said.

"Did people see her fall?" Bennett asked.

"Not many, but some. She graciously stood and waved to those who had and made her way to the carriage, making a jest as she went. It wasn't until she was seated again that we noticed the swelling. I called in her private physician straight away."

Bennett eyed the two men. "The people already believe her too young and inexperienced to lead. It would be damaging to allow her to be seen limping and injured. This will only serve in weakening her reputation."

"Precisely, which is why I've already arranged for Her Majesty to be taken somewhere until she heals," Potterfield said. "She needs to be away from the prying eyes of London and the new palace."

"And in the meantime what are people to be told?" Bennett asked. "I doubt it will help her reputation if the Queen takes a holiday."

"That is why we are here." Potterfield took a seat and motioned to Ellis. "After the incident, Ellis had an idea worth investigating and it would seem you were correct. Your cousin looks remarkably like Her Majesty."

"A stand-in?" Bennett asked, understanding now why Ellis had pointed her out. There was no possible way for that woman to pose as Queen Victoria.

"You intend to have a simple country miss charade as the Queen?" Bennett asked. "That's ridiculous."

"She's quite amiable," Ellis said. "And intelligent. I can assure you, Evelyn is up to the task."

"We would compensate her for the time she provides," Potterfield said.

Bennett couldn't believe the discussion. He was nearly on probation with the Brotherhood for following his instincts rather than orders, and yet they were going to bring in a girl who was barely gentry to impersonate the queen! The whole notion seemed asinine. He'd made no apologies for his methods. While they might be unorthodox, they often worked, even if they did stray from direct orders. This was madness. How could the man who was constantly criticizing Bennett's unorthodox methods believe this was a good idea? Obviously it was up to Bennett to be the voice of reason.

"She is trustworthy? This is a most delicate situation," Bennett said. "Think of the consequences if this ruse is unsuccessful. We can't afford to have some girl go half-cocked and start spreading rumors about the queen or the palace or anything that takes place within its walls."

"Evelyn is not a gossip," Ellis said. "Trust me, she is perfect for this assignment."

"We can use the girl for the Belgium opera performance and the people will be none the wiser," Potterfield said. "She won't need to speak, merely make an appearance. It will buy us some time for Her Majesty to heal and then we can proceed as usual."

"How will she know how to behave properly? This is the queen we're speaking of. Not any woman can stand in her place and behave accordingly," Bennett said.

"Precisely why you're here, Somersby." Potterfield gave him a toothy grin. "You will train her and be her escort. Were you not already planning to attend that opera with her?"

"With Victoria, yes, she is my cousin," Bennett said.

"Then nothing has changed with that," Potterfield said.

He felt as if the world had turned inside out. He steered clear of proper Society as much as possible, yet he was the one chosen to teach the girl manners. "She is a woman." One to whom Bennett had felt the powerful pull of attraction. This would never work. "Do you not think someone who is more genteel would be better for the task? Someone who is better with women?"

"Who would you suggest? Morton? He is the best among us with women, if that is the only requirement," Ellis said.

"Morton is a fool," Bennett said, flexing his fingers and then clenching them into fists.

"Precisely," Potterfield said. "You were selected."

"I don't know the first thing about training women."

"Can't see that it could be more difficult than the training you do at Argyll."

Their annual training exercises in Scotland covered everything from weaponry skills to extreme riding conditions, while Bennett himself had always been the lead trainer for hand fighting and proper defense. "I don't see how teaching gentlemen the necessary skills to protect the monarch prepares me for this. Is Ellis to instruct her on his horse acrobatics as well?"

"Somersby, enough. This is not up for conversation or negotiation," Potterfield said. "You will do this." With that, he came to his feet.

Bennett could knock the man down with little more than a shove, yet he had to defer to his authority if he wanted to be a working member of the Brotherhood.

"Ellis, it is up to you to persuade your uncle to agree to this, tell them whatever you have to, but do not disclose the Queen's injury. Somersby, you will work with her, teach her what she needs to know to pass as Queen for the Belgium opera." Potterfield patted Bennett on the shoulder. "I shall make arrangements for you to be brought into the Queen's cabinet so you have easy access to Miss Marrington. In the meantime, Lynford will go with me tomorrow as we settle Her Majesty in her new location. The two of us will be the only ones who know of her whereabouts. To keep things safe."

"You are bringing the priest with you?" Ellis asked.

"She is still unmarried," Potterfield said.

"Her reputation will most assuredly be safe with Lynford then," Bennett said. "Those foolish oaths of his."

"Now then, I am going to head back to London." Potterfield looked pointedly at Bennett. "You will follow your orders, understood?"

"Understood," Bennett said. Technically Bennett outranked Potterfield, at least in the aristocracy, but here in the Brotherhood, Potterfield was in charge and he doled out the orders as best he saw fit.

Bennett knew Potterfield was punishing him for "disregarding orders." Still, Bennett maintained he made his choices for good reasons. He had excellent instincts, and compliant or not, his calls had been the right ones on more than one occasion.

After Potterfield left, Bennett and Ellis agreed to change and meet back downstairs. If Bennett was to be working with the girl, he'd need to observe her, see what he was up against.

Twenty minutes later Bennett was on his way downstairs, clean and in dry clothes, clothes that were not exactly meant for a ball, regardless of it being in the country. He did not intentionally engage Society more than his work required of him. He'd been raised in it so he was perfectly capable of tutoring any young chit on the manners and expectations of the queen's court, but it was an absurd waste of his talents.

"I don't know about you, but I feel a hell of a lot better in dry clothes," Ellis said from behind him. The man was shorter by nearly a head. "Shall we?" He led them over to where his cousins stood.

Bennett did his best to keep his eyes off Evelyn Marrington; instead, he focused his attention on her father, Sir Marrington.

"Cousins," Ellis said, inclining his head to the women with a fond smile. "Uncle." He shook the older man's hand, then bent over his aunt's hand. "Aunt."

"Ellis, I do hope you're well," Sir Marrington said.

"Indeed," he said jovially.

"My dear nephew, do not be rude and deprive us an introduction to your handsome friend." Mrs. Marrington smiled up at Bennett, then gave a curtsy, her manner simpering.

"Bennett Haile, Earl of Somersby, my aunt, Lucinda Marrington, and her daughters." He spoke their names, but the one who held his attention was Miss Evelyn Marrington.

Bennett bowed his head, but before he could say anything, Mrs. Marrington pushed herself forward, both physically and conversationally.

"Dear nephew, have you forgotten that my dear Portia recently married the Viscount Handlebrook? And it will be news to you that our Jillian is newly betrothed to the Earl of Bellview." She smiled at Bennett, her gaze gleaming with calculated intent. "Our Evelyn hasn't made her match yet."

He allowed his eyes to fall to Evelyn Marrington. Her whiskey-colored eyes locked on his and the intelligence shining there drew him in, the proverbial moth to the flame. He'd always been attracted to clever women, but he knew from experience they were the most dangerous. Silly and foolish girls could be irritating, but they did not have the skills to be cunning.

Miss Evelyn Marrington's eyes were not her only fine feature. Her blazing hair fought against the constraints she'd put it into, the vibrant ringlets framing her face. Her figure was the soft and curvy kind that made him want to lock them in his bedchamber and explore every delicious inch.

The woman in question rolled her eyes. "Mother, please," she hissed. Her delicate complexion did nothing to hide her embarrassment, and it only increased as they stood there in awkward silence. Mrs. Marrington was waiting—

apparently—for him to drop to one knee and instantly propose to her middle daughter. Miss Marrington looking as though she was waiting for the ground to open up and swallow her.

For a moment he was tempted to dust off his rusty manners, step forward, and put her out of her misery by asking her to dance. He ruthlessly squelched the urge. He refused to indulge Mrs. Marrington's fantasies that he might make an appropriate suitor, or Miss Marrington's for that matter. Although her mother's pushiness clearly embarrassed her, the interest in her gaze was unmistakable. No, neither of them needed encouragement, and he certainly didn't need to break the girl's toes before they brought her to London.

"May I have this dance, dear cousin?" Ellis asked.

Miss Marrington hesitated for an instant and her mother, entirely lacking in grace, nudged her. "Evelyn, don't be daft, dear," her mother said.

Evelyn blinked her eyes slowly, and it seemed she suddenly became aware of her mother and cousin.

Ellis held his arm out and she reluctantly took it, disappearing into the crowd on the dance floor.

Only then did Bennett take a breath.

Chapter Two

"Ellis, what are you doing here in Epping? You rarely visit and you certainly have never brought guests," Evelyn asked once they began their dance.

"Can a man not come out to see his favorite cousins?" he asked.

"I suppose, but you don't. Or you have not until tonight."

He chuckled. "You are a suspicious sort." Then he gave a slight shrug. "Though I suppose in this situation your suspicions are not unwarranted. I came to speak with you."

Ellis was five years her senior, which was just enough that they'd never been particularly close, and while they'd always been friendly, she could think of absolutely no reason why he would want to talk her alone.

Did it have something to do with Lord Somersby? Was Ellis conspiring to marry her off, too? She looked in the direction where the earl had previously stood, but he was gone. A pang of disappointment shot through her. Not that she wanted to pursue anything with him, but he was a feast for the eyes. He had a face and form the likes of which she rarely had the opportunity to appreciate.

She swallowed and nodded. "Very well. Perhaps we should walk instead of dance."

"Excellent idea." He led her off the dance floor, then looked back to where they'd left his travel companion with her family. "Bennett will likely have my head for leaving him there with your mother and sisters, but I have something to discuss with you in private."

Private. In her experience there were only two reasons she was ever called in for a private discussion. The first because her mother was disappointed in her lack of interest in securing a good match, and the second because her father wanted her to know that her mother was a nervous sort and to not heed her warnings. Evie didn't think her cousin wanted to talk about either of those things. "This all sounds so mysterious, Ellis. Do hurry and tell me, as you're making me quite nervous," Evelyn said.

He chuckled. He maneuvered them to a quiet corner, far from the crowd. "Have you ever heard any rumors about me?"

She eyed him a moment, trying to gauge if his question was sincere. How was she supposed to answer that? It was not in her nature to be dishonest, but much of what she'd heard about her cousin was so sensationalized. "I suppose, nothing too salacious though. Merely about your past time." She gave him a reassuring smile. "And that you are an excellent rider."

"That I am." He glanced around them. "The others—are they about me working for the Crown?"

Her eyes narrowed. "Some ancient organization, I've heard." She waved her hand dismissively. The stories she'd heard whispered seemed so outside the realm of believability, she didn't dare whisper them aloud for fear he would laugh at her. Besides, she didn't want Ellis to think she was a simpleton to listen to such gossip. "Sounds fairly preposterous to me."

"It is true. I do, in fact, work for a secret organization for the Crown."

She opened her mouth, then closed it when he nodded.

"While I cannot give you many details, suffice it to say that much of what you've probably heard is true. And it would seem that we find ourselves in need of some assistance. Very particular assistance." Chagrin flickered across his face. "From you."

Her heart stuttered. Unless they needed an awkward country miss, it seemed unlikely she had anything to offer them. "From me? Whatever could I do?"

"That I cannot tell you, at least not yet. I merely need you to understand that your country needs you. Are you amenable?"

She held up a hand. "So you've told me that you work for a secret government agency, though you can give me no details about it. And now you have some cryptic assignment for me, but can give me no details about that either."

"More or less."

"Will it be dangerous?" Her breath caught as she considered the possibility.

They stepped out of the ballroom and onto a large balcony overlooking Lady Fenwick's gardens, nearly colliding with Lord Somersby.

"Perfect," Ellis said, turning Evie over to the earl.

"Wait, Ellis," she said. "What do you—?"

"Somersby will explain," Ellis said as he made a quick departure around the corner and back into the ballroom.

The earl's muscles tightened beneath her hand, reminding her that she'd fallen into the man's arms and still hadn't righted herself. She looked up at him, feeling slightly tongue-tied, not something she was terribly accustomed to. Abruptly she moved away. She rarely had contact with anyone but the local gentry, and Somersby was nothing like them. He was nothing like any local man Evie had ever met, which was perfectly absurd.

"Am I to believe you are one of Ellis's cohorts?" she asked.

His scowl deepened. "Cohorts? What do you mean?"

"Accomplices."

"That word does imply nefarious—"

"You know what I mean, Lord Somersby. Are you one of my cousin's *professional* associates?"

He hesitated for an almost imperceptible instant. "Yes."

"And that is why you are here?"

He nodded.

"To… to recruit me for some secret purpose?" When she said it aloud, it sounded far more exotic than anything Ellis had said. Excitement surged through her. This man, with his imposing size and constant frown, might represent the only adventure she ever had.

He glanced around the balcony. A few couples walked together, arm in arm, or with the lady's hand quite properly placed upon her escort's sleeve, as was Evie's. She looked again at her gloved hand draped onto his forearm. When had she placed it there? She hadn't. Obviously he had done that and she had missed it entirely.

"This is not the best time or place to discuss the mission, Miss Marrington."

Her strange musings stopped mid-thought as she realized there would never be a time or place for her to speak privately with Lord Somersby. Even now her mother must be beside herself with anticipation of an imminent proposal. She needed to get away from Somersby before anyone else drew any conclusions, either. "It must be now or never, my lord."

He pulled her to a slightly more secluded area. "A situation of national importance has arisen, and we…well, we need a woman to assist us in dealing with it."

He was so very earnest, and Evie found that incredibly attractive. No one ever took her seriously, not even her father, though she knew he loved her dearly.

"What would you have me do?" she found herself asking. "I have no special skills, unless you need something written, but certainly men in your positions could find someone with more experience in that area."

"Written?"

She frowned up at him. Obviously he did not know what she was talking about. "My lord, if my cousin did not tell you about my writing, if he even knows about it, I do not see what I can possibly—"

"I am not free to disclose the nature of our mission, Miss Marrington. I don't even believe it is a good idea." He cast a disparaging glance toward the door through which Ellis had made his exit.

With an odd feeling of regret, Evie took her hand from Somersby's sleeve and took a step back. "Then perhaps you and my cousin ought to discuss it further before you approach me again."

"No, no. This has come out all wrong," Somersby said impatiently. "You were chosen by the senior-most agent in the…the association. You are particularly suited to the task. Even your cousin agrees."

"Then what—"

Somersby grabbed her suddenly, hugging her to his chest as he spun her around and shoved her toward a corner of the balcony. A huge piece of clay pottery shattered on the ground next to him, though his shoulder did not escape unscathed.

"Are you all right?" he asked, his tone gruff but concerned.

She looked up at him in astonishment. Had he not moved so quickly, she'd have been crushed. As it was, he'd saved her.

• • •

Miss Marrington was shaking in Bennett's arms. He did not blame her. How would anyone anticipate such a dramatic turn of events at a country ball? Lord Fenwick ought to be throttled for allowing the condition of his home to create such risks for his guests. Hell, even for his family.

People began scurrying about them, but Bennett only felt the subtle tremor of her body. She was like a small bird, far too delicate for him, yet somehow she fit perfectly in his arms.

"Oh my dear, Evelyn!" her mother cried, prying her away from him. She and Sir Marrington led Evie away from the crowd that had gathered, but her father stopped suddenly and returned to Bennett, clasping his hand and shaking it vigorously.

"Thank God for you, my lord," Marrington said. "Thank God for you."

Bennett looked up at the roof above them just as Ellis returned. "What do you suppose happened?" Ellis asked.

"Damned if I know."

"A calculated attempt on your life?"

"Doubtful," Bennett drawled. "More like a miscalculated schedule of house maintenance."

"I suppose I should thank you for saving my cousin. It is a damned good thing you were here with her."

"Yes, well, I wouldn't have been had you not shoved her at me earlier, but you're welcome nonetheless." He had to admit that saving her had been one thing, but getting a taste of her in his arms had been quite another. Miss Marrington was definitely proving to be rather tempting. He might not always toe the line, as it were, when it came to propriety and rules, but he knew better than to tangle with a chaste country miss.

It was then that Bennett noticed that Evelyn Marrington was surrounded by her entire family, her gaggle of sisters fretting and swooning.

"Well? What do you think of her? Of Evie?"

He thought she was a distraction—a tempting, delectable distraction. "Does it actually matter what I think of her?"

Ellis grinned. "No, I don't suppose it does. Potterfield has spoken."

"Indeed." It seemed he was going to be up to his neck in one particular flame-haired beauty, at least for a few weeks.

• • •

Evie barely glimpsed Lord Somersby before her parents whisked her and her sisters back inside the ballroom. They were not about to risk another mishap of falling exteriors.

She was ready to retire for the evening, but her mother insisted she remain for at least three additional songs to assure people that she had come out of the balcony incident unscathed. Besides, according to her mother, the ordeal had brought attention to her, and with all those bachelors in attendance, Evie couldn't waste the opportunity.

Why couldn't they understand that she had a different course in mind for her life? She loved children, of course, but could not envision herself as a mother, much less a wife. And how was she to join the ranks of such writers as Mary Shelley, or Jane Austen, if she was prevented from pursuing her writing?

Evie wanted to be an author. Her mind swam with thoughts and insights on the condition of men, women, and society. Would a husband allow her to pursue her passion? Would a man like Somersby share his wife with—?

Dear heaven. Where did that thought come from? Likely from the fact that she could see the brooding earl all the way across the ballroom; he towered over the rest of the guests. Her cousin left Somersby and sauntered across to where she and her family gathered.

"May I have a word with you, Evie… Ah, Evelyn?" Ellis asked.

Her mother chortled; her tittering laugh grated on Evie's nerves. Their matriarch shepherded the other Marrington girls away. "Time for refreshments, ladies." She placed her closed fan on Ellis's arm. "Do let us know, nephew, if we have celebrating to do." She eyed Evie, then they were strolling across the ballroom to the refreshments table.

"What was that about?" Ellis asked once the rest of their family had left them.

"My mother has hopes for me, and she believes you are the resolution of those hopes, or at the very least that you've brought him here."

Ellis looked as though he would choke.

"Do not worry," Evie said. "She has convinced herself, on more than one occasion, that a suitor was interested." She'd been handling her mother for quite some time and would do so again.

Ellis nodded knowingly. "Somersby is, as far as I know, a confirmed bachelor. Perhaps I should have told her as much."

"It wouldn't have mattered. She accuses me of having my head in the clouds, but she's the one with the ridiculous imaginings."

Ellis chuckled.

"Now then, did we have more to discuss? Can you give me any more information on this 'mission' you need help with?"

"Not much," Ellis said. "We need you to accompany us to London where you will be told all you need to know."

Evie studied Ellis for a moment, taking in the crease between his brows and the pensive set of his shoulders. "I asked you earlier if it will be dangerous, but you shoved me off on Lord Somersby. Is that your way of telling me it shall be dangerous?"

"No, of course not. I would not put you in such a position."

"Oh. Well, that's a relief." Nevertheless, she still felt the strangest little pang of disappointment. It wasn't that she wanted to be in danger. It was merely that thus far in her life, nothing interesting had ever happened to her. "Ellis, how am I to decide with so little information?"

"You will just have to trust me."

"And Lord Somersby."

"Well, yes. You will have the most contact with him during this whole thing."

"I am not certain what am I supposed to say to all this. A secret mission, no information beforehand, dealing with Lord Somersby…"

"You say yes." He squeezed her shoulder. "Or at least say that you will think on it tonight. Give me your answer tomorrow. But we truly need you, Cousin."

"Is Lord Somersby always so quick?"

"I beg your pardon?"

"When we were on the balcony," she said. "He moved so fast, I hardly knew what was happening."

Ellis coughed into his hand. "Yes. He is one of our most effective operatives."

"So he is often put into dangerous situations?"

"Yes, of course."

"But this particular situation is not dangerous?"

Ellis's mouth moved in an attempt to form words, but no sound came out.

"Ellis?"

"You can trust Somersby to keep you safe should the need arise."

"Hm."

"Do you have additional questions?"

"Other than what I'd be doing, specifically?"

"Yes, other than that," he said.

"No, I don't suppose so." All her questions seemed to be

about Lord Somersby, and it would be entirely inappropriate to interrogate Ellis about his companion. She supposed Ellis might not even know him well. "I shall think on your offer this evening and let you know my answer tomorrow."

Although she believed she had already decided. If nothing else, this little adventure could stoke her imagination and give her material for her writing. She refused to entertain the possibility that spending time with Lord Somersby was part of her reason for accepting the task. It wasn't because of the way she'd felt when he'd pulled her into his arms.

Or was it?

It had felt incredibly intimate. Men didn't embrace women they'd just met. A strict protocol was always observed, and yet Lord Somersby had disregarded it. To save her life, of course, but still. Another man might have merely pushed her out of the way.

Somersby was obviously not a conventional man. Evie caught sight of him returning to the drawing room ahead of Lord Fenwick, practically into the arms of Lady Dawson, the wife of Viscount Dawson, and a most annoying woman.

"If you'll excuse me, Evie, I believe one of your neighbors is attempting to foist her daughter off on Somersby and your mother is about to fend her off with a chair. If I don't rescue him soon, there may be blood."

Evie found herself smiling at the notion of the large and powerful Lord Somersby being coerced into doing anything he did not want to do. "I believe I've had enough excitement for one night, Ellis. Pray, do not let any other untoward thing happen to your companion tonight." She took advantage of her mother's distraction with Lady Dawson and her daughter to sneak out of the ballroom.

She managed to get to the bedroom she was to share with her sister, and methodically readied herself for bed. She craved the silence of her own thoughts for the remainder of the evening, and not merely to consider the request Ellis had made.

Getting away from her family for a time on a reasonably safe adventure was more than tempting. She'd wanted to say yes immediately, regardless of what the assignment was.

The thought of escaping her mother's aggressive husband hunting was incredibly tempting. And the presence of Lord Somersby was certainly no deterrent; though, Evie knew better than to allow her curiosity about him to dictate her decision. She wondered what was behind that brooding visage, what made him so serious. He didn't seem quite as convinced that she would be able to assist them in their mission, which was really the deciding factor. Evie intended to prove to him, as well as herself, that she could accomplish whatever she set her mind to.

• • •

Ellis had assured Bennett that his impressions from the night before had more to do with their disruptive entrance than the realities of the Marrington family. Intruding upon a country house party at Lord Fenwick's estate had not been part of Bennett's plan. But when they'd first ridden up to Marrington House, they'd been sent thirty miles further west to find the entire family attending a ball at the local earl's estate.

As he'd stood in the corridor dripping on the Fenwick's rug, everyone in the drawing room had gone quiet, surreptitiously eyeing him. He might be taller and broader than most men, and one would think he'd have become accustomed to the stares and whispers of people who saw him for the first time. It seemed he never could escape their curious gazes, but he could take it. Unfortunately, his poor sister could not. She was only an inch shy of his height, and gangly as well. He'd learned a long time ago to avoid Society and their silly, superficial attitudes. They had cost him his sister.

Damnation. He wasn't here to ruminate on the terrible slights Christy had suffered at Society's hands. He had a job to do, and he really needed to obey orders this time. He couldn't defy Potterfield's command once more and still remain in the Brotherhood, even if the old man still seemed to dwell in the previous decade.

Last night Ellis had whisked Miss Marrington away to speak with her privately and then she'd disappeared. He really needed to speak to her at length, needed to see whether she was up to the task Potterfield expected him to accomplish.

She had backbone, he'd give her that, and perhaps a streak of adventurousness. She'd been shaken by the incident on the balcony, but she'd also been curious, looking up at the roof from where the huge piece of stone had fallen. Had her parents not whisked her away, he was certain she'd have stayed and asked questions about the incident.

Even so, the idea of substituting her for Victoria was ridiculous. He could not see how they would ever get away with it. Miss Marrington did not possess the sophistication of a London debutante, and certainly had none of the polish of Court. Her eyes were guileless, and her mouth…so plush and pink…was too quick to smile, to question, to fascinate.

All right, so she did resemble Victoria. Slightly. In stature only. Perhaps a bit in facial features, too, the way siblings might appear similar. But that flaming red hair was impossible. It made him think absurd thoughts, like how it would look spread about her on a silken pillow, whether it would feel as soft as it appeared, if the smooth wisps about her face would curl tightly around his fingers.

She'd been blessed with curves, too, and Bennett had awakened more than once during the night remembering the lush bounty he'd felt beneath the bodice of her gown when he'd pressed her against him on the balcony.

Good God. This mission was making him a simpleton.

He ordered his thoughts, straightened his waistcoat, and made his way downstairs in hopes of finding breakfast. It was early enough that the dining room should be relatively free of guests. The empty corridors gave him hope that he'd be able to break his fast in peace and quiet. The aroma of fresh cooked meats and bread led the way, indicating that even though it was an early hour, the staff was prepared for Fenwick's guests to eat.

He had already opened the door when he heard the guests' lively chatter. If he wanted a quiet breakfast, he was not going to find it here. And to make matters worse, women, all animatedly speaking over one another, surrounded the table.

This would never work, and he decided to say as much to Pennington as soon as possible. The Brotherhood couldn't share a valuable national secret with even one of them. With any luck, Miss Marrington would refuse the assignment, and Bennett could come up with another plan for Pennington. Because in truth there was no reason for Miss Mannington to put herself out for a purpose that had not been explained to her.

"Come in, my lord," a voice beckoned.

Every instinct in his body insisted he turn and flee the room, and he did exactly that just as Lady Fenwick arrived. "Lord Somersby! I see you are an early riser, too. Come in, come in!"

There was no turning back now, not when she threaded her arm through the crook in his elbow and pushed through to the breakfast room. Sadly, there was no legitimate excuse that would allow him to turn around, so he closed the door behind him.

The woman who had first called to him smiling broadly was Mrs. Marrington.

Bennett nodded and tried to ignore the staring eyes of the people around the table. Three of the Marrington daughters sat near their mother, and all four women watched his every step as he made his way across the dining room.

The heat from their stares burned into his back as he stood at the sidebar and loaded his plate. He had not felt such attention since his father died and he'd assumed the Earldom. He'd been arrogant and foolhardy back then and enjoyed the attention from the eligible maidens and their mothers. Then he'd met Gwyneth and learned how truly deceptive they could be.

He took more time than was necessary selecting foods for his plate, knowing full well he would not eat everything.

"As I was saying, I still think that if our monarch was a man, none of this would have happened," Mrs. Marrington finally said.

Bennett was nearly ready to take his seat, but the words

stopped him.

"She is young and inexperienced, but we should give her a chance, she is our queen," Miss Marrington's sister said.

He could not stand here any longer without drawing undue attention to himself, so he turned and took his place at the far end of the table.

"What are your thoughts on our new queen, Lord Somersby? She is awfully young to be weighted with such important duties," Mrs. Marrington said. "And unmarried at that." She clicked her tongue disapprovingly.

"Indeed she is." He smeared butter on a chunk of bread. "But she was raised knowing she would be queen and therefore has had time to prepare," he said.

"Have you met her?" one of the Marrington girls asked, this one delicate and fair.

"She is my cousin," he said simply.

The girl's eyes widened and he looked down at his breakfast. That should end the gossip about Victoria, at least while he was in the room.

"What brings you to Essex?" Mrs. Marrington asked.

"A travel companion to your nephew. Nothing more."

"It is lovely countryside, I do hope you'll have time to explore," she said.

"Unfortunately, we're leaving today." He did his best to be polite, but beneath the scrutiny of the Marrington women, he was losing his patience. None of them looked at his face, but rather seemed entirely enthralled by the breadth of his shoulders and the volume of food on his plate—all except for Evelyn. Her flaming wild hair was pulled back in some sort of modest confection, but curls still teased her cheeks. She did not look at him at all.

Mrs. Marrington clicked her tongue. "Perhaps another visit then. It is really quite lovely. I'm certain one of my daughters could show the two of you around."

"Leave the man alone, Eleanor." It was Sir Marrington, who quickly shuttered his annoyed expression and went to the sideboard for his breakfast.

Bennett nodded to him, but the man was not allowed to take his plate in peace.

"I was merely being hospitable," Mrs. Marrington said. "It is quite unfortunate to be in a new part of the country and not have a guide to show one around."

The door opened and two more Marrington daughters entered with Ellis. Well, they were a family of early risers.

"Uncle, might I have a word?" Ellis asked.

"Indeed." He set his plate back on the sideboard, then followed the younger man, leaving Bennett in the dining room with only the Marrington women for company. This was the second time he had done this in two days. Bennett would box Ellis's ears for this later.

"My lord, 'tis very nice of you to join us this morning," the eldest Marrington sister said. She was tall and willowy with strawberry blond hair and a wide smile. He vaguely remembered Ellis telling him their names, but at the moment he remembered only Evelyn's. She was the one that mattered for this assignment so that was all he was concerned with.

"I do believe it has stopped raining," another said.

Evelyn sat at the far end of the table and resumed reading a book that was propped open in front of her.

"Evelyn, dear, perhaps you could read another time. We have a guest," Mrs. Marrington said.

"Mother, we are all guests here at Fenwick Hall," Evelyn

said.

Her mother frowned and Bennett hid a smile. She had bite, that one. Perhaps she was inhospitable and didn't realize it. The aloofness would serve her well posing as the queen. All royalty were aloof, untouchable, though Victoria was not like that on her own. In public, she had mastered the behavior at an early age.

"You said you were leaving today, my lord, returning to London?" the eldest sister asked.

"After a quick diversion to my estate, yes."

"And where might that be?" Mrs. Marrington asked.

"Berkshire. It is not too far from here, only a few hours ride."

"Is it a harsh land?"

"No, it is quite lovely," he said.

"Is that not where Windsor Castle is, My Lord?" one of the Marrington sisters asked.

"It is." He paused a moment, then asked, "Miss Marrington, I wonder if I could inquire as to what you're reading?"

Silence fell over the room and all eyes turned to Evelyn. He simply wanted to see her behavior. Thus far he'd been so unimpressed with the Marrington family that he was highly reluctant to take her anywhere.

She looked up slowly, met his face. There it was again, that intelligence sparking in her eyes. He was too far away from her right now, but he knew from the night before that they were a warm amber color. "Frankenstein." She immediately went back to reading.

Her sister nudged her and Evelyn looked up. A silent conversation seemed to flow between the two women before Evelyn looked back at him. "Have you read it, my lord?"

"Yes."

Surprise rounded her eyes. "Indeed? And what did you think?" A smile teased at her pink lips.

"I did not care for it."

She frowned. "Why ever not?"

"Evelyn," her mother hissed, then shook her head.

"It is a legitimate question. It's a nearly perfect piece of literature," Evelyn said.

He could tell her why. He'd spent the entire novel feeling far too similar to the monster and his plight in Society, but he'd be damned if he'd ever admit that to anyone, especially a roomful of gossiping females. "I believe Mary Shelley is a gifted writer, but the book simply did not appeal to me."

She returned to reading, satisfied that she had met whatever requirement her family had placed on her.

He stood and nodded to them all. "I wish you ladies a good day." Then he turned on his heel and walked out. He stood just outside the door listening.

"Evie, that is not how you interest a gentleman," one of the sisters said.

"Honestly, child, I simply do not know what we shall do with you. I suppose your father and I will have to select your husband since we cannot rely on you to do so, though we might have to sew your mouth shut."

• • •

Bennett left the dining area and went in search of Ellis. The story they were telling the Marringtons was that Ellis's mother had fallen ill and had requested Evelyn to come and keep her company while she healed. But Bennett had his doubts about the plan, and he intended to make his objections known as soon as possible.

The Marrington women were gossips, which meant they could not be trusted. He'd had the opportunity to observe them after Evelyn had retired, and knew that they had discussed him at length. They'd discussed every other guest as well, although the conjectures about his own family, his estate, and his annual income were the most disturbing. He would have none of it, not after the way such insensitive talk had destroyed his sister.

He came upon Ellis just as the man stepped out of Fenwick's library. His uncle followed and jovially patted the man on his back, nodded to Bennett, then headed back to the dining room.

"Everything is set," Ellis said.

"This is never going to work," Bennett said. "We need to leave now."

"What do you mean? Even Potterfield thought she was perfect," Ellis said.

They walked to the back of the house and out the French doors that opened to the gardens. "I do not mean to disrespect your family, but they have done nothing but whisper about me and many others since we walked in. Discretion is quite obviously not among their virtues. We could never expect her to hold such an important matter in confidence." He frowned. "Why am I the only one concerned about this?"

"Yes, my aunt and some of my cousins are likely discussing you. My aunt is quite…enthusiastic about marrying off her daughters. But none of that is relevant to this situation. Besides the fact, Evie is quite different from her mother and sisters."

"They were gossiping about the Queen this morning at breakfast," Bennett said.

Ellis released a slow breath. "Precisely why we need Evie to come to London. People will only gossip more and more if Victoria is not seen, or worse if people see her injured. You said yourself that she cannot afford for people to see her weakened."

"That does not mean that this is the solution," Bennett said. "We could simply have her out of the public eye for a week or more."

"It is not for you or I to make this decision," Ellis said. "Certainly you must have recognized that Potterfield is not pleased with you as of late."

"Of course I have noticed that. He'd tightening the leash as if I am an untrained pup. None of my decisions have ever resulted in anyone save myself getting injured."

"No, but they could have." Ellis sighed. "I'm not suggesting you are wrong, but for a while, work with Potterfield, follow his orders and eventually he'll start focusing on someone else. But if you're not careful, he'll remove you, you'll be down with the likes of Morton." Ellis patted his back and grinned. "Tell me you've seen the resemblance between Evie and our dear monarch."

Ellis was right. Bennett knew that. Still, the whole situation infuriated him. Bennett shrugged. "I have. I will not deny that she favors Her Majesty. Except for her hair." Not to mention her sinful curves, but he would refrain from discussing that matter with Ellis.

"We can hide her hair."

"Still. This will not work and it's exceedingly dangerous to bring a civilian into our work."

"I understand your concerns, but we don't have any choice in the matter. Potterfield made his orders quite clear."

Bennett eyed Ellis. "We could tell him the chit said no, that she refused to come along with us."

"Allow me to remind you that if you disobey Potterfield again, your future in the Brotherhood will be dismal. He will likely place you on guard duty at Buckingham Palace."

He stood there thinking on what Ellis said. Damnation, but the man was right. If he weren't so bloody ambitious, then none of this would matter, but it did matter. He not only wanted to retain his membership in the Brotherhood, he wanted to succeed Potterfield in the Brotherhood, and that depended on the man's opinion of him. At the moment that opinion was rather low.

"Imagine, though, if you bring her to London and you teach her what she needs to do to successfully pull off this charade. Potterfield will have little to say to you other than praise."

"Doubtful." But Ellis's thought had merit. Bennett swore. "What are we to do about her hair?"

Ellis popped him on the back and urged him forward. "We'll think of something. Now to convince her."

Bennett stopped walking. "She hasn't agreed yet?"

"No, but I suspect she won't be nearly as difficult as you."

A large tree ahead housed a swing and there sat the woman, her red curls piled onto her head.

"Evelyn," Ellis said.

She looked up from a book and met her cousin's face. She smiled, came to her feet. "I have considered your offer."

"And?"

Bennett took in the woman's features. There were

similarities between Evelyn and Victoria—the shape of their eyes, the cheekbones, the thin aristocratic nose, but this woman was far prettier than Victoria.

"I accept," she said cheerfully. Her glance strayed to his before she quickly averted her eyes.

"Splendid," Ellis said. He nudged Bennett with his elbow. "I told you she was perfect."

"I wouldn't go that far, but under the circumstances, she'll do," Bennett said. "I shall take her."

Chapter Three

Evie whirled on Ellis again. "I'm not certain what gives you the idea that I am yours to sell into marriage, but I will have none of it." She crossed her arms over her chest. She supposed she should count herself fortunate that he was handsome and young and wealthy. Still, she didn't want to marry; she wanted to be a novelist. The authoress Jane Austen had never married, she'd considered her work her marriage and Evelyn wanted to do the same. But it would seem as if she had no say in the manner.

"What the devil is she talking about?" Lord Somersby asked. "No one is selling anyone into marriage."

She allowed his words to settle into her and relief washed over her. "Oh, thank goodness."

Lord Somersby's right brow rose.

Blush burned her cheeks. "My apologies, but based on what you said, I assumed that you were taking me for a wife, albeit not enthusiastically."

His eyes rounded. "I have no need for a wife."

"Well, there was certainly no way for me to know that. I mean you are infinitely preferable to Lord Edgerly, but still I have no intentions of marrying anyone."

Lord Somersby shook his head. "Why are we even discussing this?"

"Neither one of you have been forthcoming with me on what this little adventure entails." She shrugged. "I was speculating."

"Evie, Lord Somersby is who you shall be working with on said adventure," Ellis said.

Surprise bolted through her, and something dangerously close to pleasure. "Only him? Why not you?" Ellis had told her she'd be working with Lord Somersby, but not that she'd be alone with him.

"Because Somersby here is the one for the task. That is all I can tell you now."

She felt her mouth open, and promptly closed it. She looked again at Lord Somersby, who now frowned at her, his bulky arms crossed over his wide chest. Though he dressed as a gentleman, he looked more the part of the blacksmith. "What do I need to do?"

"You come with me. No questions asked," Lord Somersby said.

Her brows rose and a sharp retort formed in her throat, but Ellis stepped forward. "Consider this, dear cousin, you shall get a reprieve from your family for a week or two and then you return. A brief holiday, if you will."

"Only me? None of the rest of them are invited?"

Lord Somersby shook his head. "Absolutely not."

She smiled. "Then whatever it is, I wholeheartedly agree."

She nudged Ellis in the ribs. "Provided you can assure me that this man isn't going to take me off to his seaside castle and chain me in a tower."

"You and your books. Real life is *not* that exciting, Evie, I keep telling you this," Ellis said. "Now then, I shall leave the two of you to get acquainted and go ready the carriage and horses." He turned to go, then stopped and looked at her. "By the by, Evie, we've told your family that my mother is ill and has requested your company while she recuperates. That is the story you shall use."

And with that she was left alone with the hulking stranger. She allowed her gaze to take in the full sight of him. She doubted she came to his shoulders. "You are exceptionally large," she said.

He said nothing, though she couldn't blame him. Her comment had done nothing but state the obvious. He'd probably heard similar hundreds of times.

"No questions? That might be difficult as I am a curious sort." Not even a hint of a smile showed on his lips. Perhaps he had no sense of humor. "Lord Somersby, my cousin has assured me that you shall protect me in the event of danger. Is that true?"

"That is a question."

She grinned. "I suppose it is."

He peered at her. "If you are going to be overly chatty, this arrangement will never work."

"Ellis suggested we should get acquainted. I was merely following instructions."

His expression barely altered. "When we arrive at my townhome, I shall give you additional details, but not until then."

Squeals came from inside the house and she ignored Catherine and Meghan waving frantically from the drawing room window. They were all smiles and giggles.

"Your family is—"

"Loud? Too much? Obnoxious?"

"Yes."

She took offense, or at least she should have taken offense, but she said nothing more. It mattered not what the Earl of Somersby thought of her family. They were not part of this agreement and he would likely never see them again.

"But what are his intensions?" she heard her mother frantically asking as Ellis and her father stepped outside the house.

Evelyn cringed. "Good heavens," she whispered.

"She's going to see my sister, dear," her father said. "Lord Somersby has naught to do with this." Then he did his best to close the door. It wouldn't matter; she'd either open it or stand so close she'd be able to hear their conversation. Ellis and her father shook hands and her father waved her to him.

She strode the length of the garden and came to his side. "Yes, Papa?"

"Are you in agreement with your cousin and wish to take this holiday?"

She faltered, uncertain if her father knew more of the truth than he let on. "Yes, I would very much prefer to go," she said quietly. A cool breeze fluttered around her, whipping curls from the confines of the braid wound onto her head.

Her sisters' voices echoed through the door. "I can't hear anything," one of them said.

Evelyn smiled. Her father looked over his shoulder,

then back at her. "Perhaps I should go along with you."

A pang of wistfulness surged through her. She would miss her family, her father the most. "They'd never survive without you," she said.

"Quite true, my dear."

Ellis rounded the corner of the house. "The carriage is ready."

Her father cleared his throat, did his best to frown in fatherly concern. "Well, then I trust that, Ellis, you shall keep her safe."

"Of course, Uncle."

Her father kissed her cheek. "Be safe, my dear, and I shall see you soon."

"I am to leave right now?" she asked. This was happening rather quickly, but she supposed if she was to live out an adventure she should be ready for nearly anything. That was what she wanted, something other than this quiet country existence to impart into her writing, her stories.

"Yes," Lord Somersby said.

"What of my clothes? I need to pack."

"It has all been taken care of. Your trunks shall meet you there," Ellis said.

"But I want to go too!" her youngest sister whined as the door flew open. Nearly three girls fell to the ground with the force; they must have all been pressed tightly to the wood with their eavesdropping.

"The carriage is around this way, Miss Marrington," a footman said.

She had no notion to what she'd just agreed to, but she waved to her family, then followed the men, setting off on her first true adventure.

Of all the arrogant men!

He wouldn't even ride with her in the carriage, instead insisting to sit in the damp weather upon his horse. Well, let him catch his death out there. She was relatively cozy inside here with a blanket wrapped around her lap. But she was expected to work with him despite having spoken to him no more than their brief and curt exchange. And her cousin had diverted away from them as soon as they'd left her village; he was headed back to London. Perhaps she should be pleased rather than offended that Lord Somersby was not accompanying her inside the carriage because then she'd have to suffer his presence in silence.

Instead, she sat in this relatively dark carriage being carted off to the Earl's London townhouse. She withdrew her notebook from her reticule and did what she did best. She made some notes for a book idea: a plucky country miss being whisked off to a cranky lord's castle where she'd be forced into a loveless marriage. Oh, and perhaps the castle had some mysterious secrets, a tower with broken stairs.

She supposed she should be mortified that she'd thought he'd wanted to marry her, and had told him so, but she generally wasn't prone to embarrassment, though her mother would have most certainly had a fit of the vapors.

Evie chuckled to herself. The whole situation was amusing. Granted, he was preferable to Lord Edgerly and his eleven children, so if this had been some sort of arranged marriage, she would have at least been pleased by her betrothed's appearance. As best, she could tell Lord

Somersby still had all of his teeth.

• • •

Bennett had opted to ride his horse rather than inside the carriage with Miss Marrington. His reasons had been twofold. He hadn't wanted to stare at her all the while imagining all manners in which to scandalize her, and he hadn't wanted to endure her peppering him with questions.

Once they'd arrived at his townhome, he'd left her to his staff to get her settled in. Mrs. Kimble, his housekeeper, had whisked the girl away. This had not been the assignment he'd been expecting, nor hoping for. He'd wanted to go to Oxford and interview the professor there who was working on a machine to send notices quickly and without the post; a telegraph machine, the man called it. Bennett felt certain that this sort of technology was precisely what the Brotherhood needed to give them an edge in protecting the Crown. Potterfield saw no reason to do things any differently than they'd been doing them for the last hundred years.

Yet, Bennett wasn't at Oxford with the professor. He was here, back in London, with Miss Marrington in tow and he was expected to transform her into the Queen, as if he were some manner of nursemaid or nanny.

His butler scratched at the door and Bennett looked up from the papers he hadn't been reading.

"There is a woman here to see you, my lord."

Another woman? Why was his life suddenly overset with women? "Who is it?"

"An old friend, she claims," Winston said.

"Send her in, but do come and relieve me if she hasn't

left in twenty minutes," Bennett said.

Winston nodded. "Very well, my lord."

Bennett stood and came around his desk to greet whomever had come to see him. He wasn't in the mood. As it was, he was concerned about having Miss Marrington at his townhome; her presence had already lifted several brows of his servants. He'd ignored their questioning glances, explaining nothing more than that she was his guest.

He eyed the door as Winston held it open and gave entrance to the tall blond beauty. Gwyneth, his former fiancée.

"You should be glad that Winston answered the door and not Mrs. Kimble. He's unfamiliar with you, but she would have refused you entrance." His housekeeper had been with him since he'd been a boy; she was more like family than servant, and she'd loathed Gwyneth.

"Is that any way to greet me, Bennett? I thought you'd be pleased to see me." She sauntered into the room, came around the desk, and propped one hip upon it.

"You thought wrong. What do you want, Gwyneth?"

She smiled, that knowing smile he'd once thought so enticing, but now he knew it hid a calculating, deceitful woman.

"You do know me, don't you, love?"

"Don't call me that. You never loved me." He shoved aside the image of her sitting atop another man.

She leaned forward, giving him a brazen view down her bodice. "I miss you. Don't you miss me? Even a little?"

Did she think him an utter fool? "No."

With graceful movements, she slid her way onto his lap, snaked her arms behind his head, and toyed with his hair. How had he ever found her blatant sensuality attractive?

She was so very different to the woman currently above stairs, in practically every way. It was almost as if they were a completely different species. Though Evelyn Marrington might look different and even behave different, with her wide eyes and country manners, Bennett had learned the hard way that women were never what they appeared to be. No matter their mood, there was always manipulation just beneath.

"I don't believe you," she purred, close to his ear. Her rosewater was cloyingly strong. "I was hoping to rekindle our romance. We never shared pleasures of the flesh and I know with you they could be so satisfying."

"Indeed."

"Oh yes."

"Interesting, because I seem to recall that when I broke off our engagement you told me you were relieved. That you'd ended up in Phillip's arms because you'd needed the affections of a man, not a beast; an oaf as large as me could surely injure such a genteel lady. I believe you also added that no woman could ever truly want me."

She frowned, her bottom lip jutted out in a ridiculous pout. "I was angry, love. I was devastated when you jilted me. I wanted to be Lady Somersby."

"You wanted my money." He stood then, effectively removing her from his lap. She caught herself before she tumbled to the floor. "Honestly, woman, I am no fool. What the devil do you want? I have neither the interest nor the time in this charade." He folded his arms over his chest. "Tell me, Gwyneth, how is your husband?"

"Broke and drunk," she said bitterly.

As well she deserved. He nodded.

Tears welled in her eyes, and if he wasn't mistaken, they were real, legitimate tears. "He is to be sent to debtor's prison."

"You want me to pay his debts?" he asked, not quite believing her nerve.

"No, of course not. I was hoping we could come to an arrangement. One that served us both." She held her arms out as if presenting herself to him. "I'm offering you my companionship in exchange for—"

"Money."

"Not precisely money. Merely a lifestyle that I have grown accustomed to living. My dowry afforded Phillip and I to live in a certain way, but then he squandered the rest of the funds. Borrowed more money than either of us ever had." She shook her head. "He is a fool."

"You are offering to be my mistress?"

"I am."

"I am not interested."

"How can you refuse me?" She took a step towards him.

"If this is truly something you need do to survive, I have no doubt there are plenty of men here in London, with fatter purses than mine, who would love to warm your bed."

"I could tell everyone about the Brotherhood."

"Which would affect your husband as well since he, too, is a member."

She waved her hand. "He has ruined himself already, but I know there are gossip rags that would pay to have a roster of members of the elite Brotherhood."

"No one knows anything of our existence, and if they do, they do not find it all that interesting."

"So you are refusing to pay me for my silence?"

"You know nothing. I have no reason to pay you." He took a step forward, allowing his full height to tower over her. He never used his size to intimidate women, but in this case, he'd make an exception. "You've been after my money from the very beginning and I caught you, saw you for what you truly were before you imprisoned me in an unfaithful marriage. This is yet another ploy to get funds from me and I don't take kindly to blackmail."

"I shall sell my information to the highest bidder."

"Do what you must."

• • •

Evelyn did her best to appear as if she were exploring the corridor of the Somersby townhome instead of eavesdropping on the earl's conversation with the pretty woman. The butler had walked by her twice and she'd pretended to be fascinated by the tapestry hanging on the wall. In truth, it was a lovely piece of work, depicting a scene where Guinevere was placed between King Arthur and Sir Lancelot, but she was more intrigued by the heated exchange coming from the earl's study.

"So you are refusing to pay me for my silence?" the woman asked.

The woman was attempting to blackmail the earl for something or another, precisely the sort of scene that would make a perfect opening for her next book. Oh, how she wished she had her notebook with her. She'd have to rely on memory and write things down once she returned to her room.

She knew the earl was speaking, she could hear the low

rumble of his voice, but he did not speak loudly enough for her to make out his words. Their exchange went back and forth for a few moments, then she heard footsteps. Evelyn slid herself next to a knight of armor. The blond woman stormed out of the earl's study and down the corridor to the front door. She halted briefly, turning around and looking in Evelyn's direction, but the armor must have hidden her well enough because the woman then left. She'd seen and heard enough to know that the woman and the earl had once been intimate. Lovers, perhaps.

Descriptions and ideas flittered through her head and she raced back up the stairs to find her notebook. She'd just stumbled onto the idea for her next book about a surly Earl who was blackmailed by a previous lover. It rang with possible intrigue and adventure, exactly what she wanted to write about.

Evelyn yawned and stretched to release the tension in her back. Shortly after she'd arisen, she'd been instructed that his lordship expected her presence in his study directly after she had breakfast, but she was tired and not moving as quickly as she normally did. She'd stayed up too late the night before working on her new book idea.

After witnessing the Earl's interaction with his visitor, Evie had been flooded with thoughts about her characters and story. She'd made several pages of notes, and even written the opening scene between a cantankerous earl and a woman blackmailing him. So far this little adventure had been what she'd needed to get her writing progressing again.

Evelyn dressed as quickly as she could, surprised and relieved to find the trunk of her belongings had been transported to her bedchamber during the night while she'd slept. Here in this grand house, sleeping in a bedchamber that was larger than the one she'd grown up sharing with one of her sisters, it was comforting to have her clothes, despite the fact that they were probably worn and out of fashion. If he wanted her to dress better for this particular venture, he'd have to purchase her some new gowns.

After downing a quick breakfast, she knocked on the earl's study door at a quarter after nine.

"Enter," he said.

She pressed the door open and stepped inside, breaching his private sanctuary much as the woman had done last night.

He looked up from the parchment upon which he was writing and assessed her. His eyes scanned the length of her and a frown settled on his brow. He beckoned her forward with a wave of his hand. "Come, we have much work to accomplish before we leave for Buckingham."

Work. So she would finally learn of what, specifically, she would be doing. She lowered herself gingerly into one of the chairs adjacent his desk, a massive, heavily carved desk of mahogany.

"Now then, I don't know if you've already deduced what you'll be doing for us, but I cannot stress enough the importance of your discretion. No one is to know, not your family, your friends, no one."

His was formidable, there was no denying that, but she felt no fear in his presence. Instead, she found herself fascinated with the lines of his face, the square angle of his jawline, and the dimple that settled deep into his chin. He was ridiculously handsome, but his expression seemed permanently locked in a scowl. She wondered what a wealthy, handsome earl had to be so angry about.

He leveled his blue eyes on her. "Understood?"

She nodded.

He stood and walked around to her. He picked up a stray curl that rested near her ear, the strand curled around his finger as a cat's tail wound around your leg when they begged for attention. She shivered against his touch. What had her cousin gotten her into?

"Have people ever told you that you resemble someone?" Earl Somersby asked.

His question nearly disappointed her, though she knew not what she'd expected. She frowned. "Once or twice I suppose."

His brows rose. "Who have they said you look like?" He moved away from her then, sat in the chair adjacent to her.

"Well, one fellow in the market said that I was the spitting image of his Aunt Gertrude, but for the most part people say I favor Her Majesty, Queen Victoria." Evie shook her head. She was loathe to admit that as she didn't want him to laugh, so she quickly added. "Personally I don't see it. Then again, I've never actually seen her, only portraits."

"You and Her Majesty are about the same age," he said.

"I am older, by two years I believe."

He nodded, leaned forward, and braced his elbows on his knees. "Miss Marrington, I need to know that I can trust your discretion."

"Yes, of course."

"I work for the Crown, as your cousin told you. I will not detail how precisely, but suffice it to say, you have been chosen to assist on a very important task. We need you to pose as Her Majesty at an upcoming event."

Had she heard him correctly? Certainly not. Charading as the monarch must be an act of treason. "I'm sorry, I thought you said that you want me to pose as the queen."

"Correct."

"Do I favor her that much?"

He eyed her, and under the weight of his scrutiny she squirmed in her chair. "You do favor her, I suppose. I am much more familiar with Her Majesty, obviously, but your features are quite similar."

No doubt Her Majesty was much prettier than she, but there had been several times when she'd been in town that people had commented on the likeness.

"There is an important traveling opera group coming in from Belgium in two days and the Queen is supposed to attend. Has something to do with the royal family there. You will only sit in her box, wave pleasantly to people, and that is all. You will not speak, merely be there in her stead."

"Yes, I can certainly do that." Then she frowned, but what if she couldn't? What if she failed? "I think I can do that. Where is the queen?"

He leaned back, crossed one long leg over the other. "That is not your concern. You need only know what is necessary for this one evening. Understood?"

"Yes."

"Now then, we'll need to go over the names of the servants, the layout of Buckingham, and your mannerisms."

"What is the matter with my mannerisms?"

"Nothing, but they are not royal. Victoria was raised to be our monarch, so she moves in a specific way."

"I see." Her mind virtually spun with thoughts, racing from one to another. She would be going into Buckingham palace, seeing parts of it that were reserved only for the royal family. "Who will know I'm there? That I'm not her?"

"Me, and perhaps one or two other members."

Which meant she had an entire palace worth of people to fool.

"And something must be done about your hair."

Had she not been so startled, she might have commented on his lack of manners. "My hair, my lord?"

"The Queen's is not so—" He frowned as if searching for the right word. "Large or red."

"I've not seen Her Majesty before, but I'd heard she was a ginger-haired as well. Is that not true?"

"Hers is more subtle. Yours will most assuredly give you away."

She hoped that didn't mean she had to cut her hair. It had always been on the wild side, curls going this way and that, and the color was closer to titian. "Will I wear her clothes?"

"Yes."

"So do you live in the palace too? Do you get to call her by her Christian name? Do you travel with Her Majesty?"

"I will not answer any of these questions."

She could see the resignation on his face. He was certainly not the one whom she could get information. She'd have to wait until the next time she saw Ellis. "Who was that woman who came here last night?" she asked abruptly.

His right brow cocked. "That is none of your concern. You are a curious sort." He was quiet for a moment as if assessing her. "Do you understand the severity of this assignment and how crucial it is that you remain absolutely silent on it? That means you can never tell anyone."

"Yes, I understand. You have mentioned as much several times already this morning. I can assure you, my lord, I might be from the country, but I am not a simpleton, nor am I a gossip."

He made a sound that was very much like a snort.

"You scoff? Why?"

"I saw your family. They were every bit as much gossips as any I've seen in London."

Handsome though he might be, the fact remained that Lord Somersby was rude and arrogant. "If you are so certain that I shall fail at this, why are you bringing me to London?" she asked.

"It is the assignment we have been given," he said, as if that explained everything.

"I beg your pardon, Lord Somersby, but I do not work for the Crown. You cannot expect me to simply do your bidding after you've done nothing but criticize my family, and me. There is absolutely nothing wrong with my hair."

"Well said, Miss Marrington," a man said from the doorway.

It was the other man she'd seen at the ball that night, but she had not been introduced to him.

Somersby came to his feet. "Potterfield. I thought you were…" He glanced at Evelyn. "Is everything all right?"

Potterfield came into the room and stood near the bookshelf across from their chairs. "That all depends on how things are going here, and it doesn't sound as if they're going very well. Somersby, did you insult this poor girl?"

The muscles along Lord Somersby's jawline twitched and his nostrils flared ever so slightly. Had she gotten the man in trouble? She did not think that noblemen could get into trouble.

"I did not insult her. I am doing what you instructed me to do. Training her in the ways of Victoria so that she can be a believable stand-in." The words seemed to inch out through his clenched teeth.

Chapter Four

"Stand and walk to the other side of the room," Bennett said.

"I beg your pardon?" Evie asked.

"I must evaluate how you walk." It was tedious and ridiculous, still Potterfield had insisted. Bennett at least was thankful that the man had left and given Bennett privacy to follow through with these orders.

She gaped at him. "How I walk?"

"Do try and keep up, Miss Marrington. People will be watching."

"Is there something wrong with how I walk?"

"Your walk is…" No. In truth, she walked with an unconscious grace and agility he found charming. There was nothing studied about her movements, nothing calculated. She managed to be both completely natural and totally bewitching, which was entirely beside the point. "Your walk is unstudied."

"Are you staying I'm clumsy?" Her gaze sparked with indignation, but perhaps a flash of pain as well. "I am well aware that I lack the grace and cultivation of my older sisters, but I assure you I am not some clumsy oaf who can't be trusted to walk into a room."

He drew in a deep breath, praying for patience. This was why he wasn't yet married. This was why he was absolutely the wrong man for this job.

"Your mannerisms must match hers," he said tightly.

She closed her eyes and took several deep breaths before standing, then walked across the room. It was not a clumsy or awkward gait, but not regal either.

"No." He shook his head. "Try it again but slower, yet with more purpose."

She crossed her arms over her ample bosom. "This is ridiculous."

He allowed his gaze to linger on her tempting curves before stepping over to her. "Miss Marrington, do you want to do this assignment or not?"

Her mouth opened, then she paused and her brows slanted down in anger. "My Lord, I realize that you are an Earl and of relation to our Queen, and our Society deems you more important than I. Perhaps they are even correct. However, it would seem to me that you," she jabbed a finger into his chest, "need me more than I need you for this assignment. Thus far you have insulted my family, the way I walk, and my hair. You are arrogant and rude and sorely lacking in manners." Her hands fisted on her hips accenting their roundedness.

How was it that this slip of a woman showed no fear of him? He'd frightened women merely by walking into their drawing room. And here he was being a bully—and for good reason—to Evelyn Marrington, but she was quite obviously not afraid of him. He couldn't help but find that both infuriating and alluring.

"You have obviously decided I do not possess the intelligence nor grace to succeed in this charade. I will not stand for this sort of treatment. I should like a carriage to bring me home on the morrow. Good day, Lord Somersby." She turned and marched from the room.

In complete disbelief, he watched her go. No one had ever spoken to him in such a way. Arrogant and rude! She was the one lacking in manners. This entire assignment echoed with idiocy. Ellis had claimed his cousin amiable and clever, neither of which Bennett had seen. All he had witnessed was her sharp tongue.

Damned if he didn't find her sass alluring as hell. All the more reason to send her back home and tell Potterfield she refused to participate. Bennett couldn't be blamed for this failure if she was the one who walked away. This would work out perfectly. He'd get to continue with the Brotherhood and not be distracted by the ridiculously attractive and fiery-tongued Miss Marrington. It would almost be worth completing the assignment just to see if she was as passionate in other areas. Almost.

• • •

Her heart was pounding so loudly she was unsure if it was indeed her heart or her boots against the stairs as she raced back to her borrowed bedchamber. Of all the infuriating men. Her mother would have fallen over dead had she heard Evie speak to him that way. "An earl, Evelyn," her mother would say, fanning off the vapors. "You might as well put me in the grave now."

She knew her harsh words had meant nothing to the Earl. She tossed some of her belongings into the trunk. The hairbrush landed with a thud. Yes, she was walking away from money that could give her the life she'd dreamed of, but no amount of coin was worth being treated as if she were daft and ugly.

More belongings tumbled into the trunk. She wondered which was more offensive, being seen as ignorant, or unattractive? Definitely the former. She had always been praised for her superior intellect, and, quite frankly, she'd never believed herself particularly attractive, especially in comparison to her sisters. But the Earl of Somersby certainly knew how to make a girl feel both.

She might not get to experience a full adventure, but the little she'd been here, she already had a book idea. Better than what she'd come with. As far as what she'd tell her mother and the rest of the family as to why she'd returned early…well, perhaps she'd come up with something tonight.

• • •

"The girl wants to return home," Bennett said as he stepped into Potterfield's study.

Potterfield looked up from his desk, but said nothing.

Bennett fully entered the room and sat in a chair across from Potterfield's massive carved desk. He shook his head regretfully. "I don't think there is any changing her mind. She's a stubborn lot."

Potterfield's eyes narrowed. "I'm trying to understand how precisely this is my problem. I believe this is your assignment. Are you forfeiting?"

"No, but I cannot be held responsible if the girl won't cooperate."

"She won't cooperate or you have made it impossible for her to do so?"

Damnation! He should have known Potterfield wouldn't simply shrug and give him leave. "Sir, it is my opinion that this assignment is too dangerous and risky for everyone involved. The girl could get hurt, and as stubborn as she is, I'm not certain I can control her."

"I never asked you to control her, Somersby. She is not a horse." He shook his head. "How is it that you know nothing about the fairer sex?"

Bennett would not answer that. He knew plenty about women and their ways. Knew about the poison of gossip and how it could destroy weaker women, as it had his sister, Christy. Knew about the greediness and deception of the stronger, cleverer of their sex and all the destruction they left in their wake. What he did not know was how to convince a strong-willed, intelligent woman to do something she'd set her mind against.

"What did you do, Somersby?"

"I did what you told me to do. She is unwilling to do as she's told."

"Be that as it may, this is your responsibility. You make this work."

"Or?" Bennett asked.

"Or you will be reclassified as a guard."

"Just like that?"

Potterfield slammed his book on the table and stood. He braced his arms on the desk and leaned forward. "You know very well that this isn't the first time you've broken protocol. Like it or not, the rules exist for a reason. You will follow them, or you will lose clearance. It is as simple as that. I will not continue to play games with you. I don't care who you are."

Bennett took a deep breath. He could walk away, end it right now, and simply be done with all of this. Then what? What would be left for him? Return to London and live the life of the idle rich? His days filled with nothing but the mindless pursuit of pleasure? Or retire to one of his country estates and live the life of a simple farmer? He didn't know which alternative seemed duller.

He knew nothing save how to be a member of the Brotherhood. It was what he'd worked toward his entire life. To walk away now would be juvenile. He refused to let a simple miss rob him of his future, no matter how alluring she was.

"Make her change her mind," Potterfield said. He walked around his desk and went to the bookshelf. "You fix this, or walk away. Your choice."

Bennett knew he'd been dismissed. Potterfield had moved on to something else and was done entertaining this conversation. So instead of being able to blame everything on Miss Marrington, Bennett had to either make her compliant, or lose everything he'd worked for. He stood and made his way out of Potterfield's study and back to his waiting steed outside.

He could find a way to make the Marrington girl stay. He'd simply offer her what most women wanted. More money.

• • •

Evie had finished packing nearly two hours before and she'd already rearranged the trunk three times. She'd tried writing some more on her book idea, but she was far too distracted with thoughts of the arrogant Lord Somersby. It was only because she was still in his townhome. Once she returned to her family's cottage, she'd be able to concentrate and get writing done. Until then she supposed she could read.

It had started to rain and the droplets knocked on the window in her bedchamber that overlooked Hyde Park. She stood at the window now, watching the moonlight blur the water rivulets as they slid down the glass. Her fingers pressed against the cool window. London. She'd wanted to come here, wanted to see the city and experience some manner of life before she resigned herself to either marriage to an unappealing older man, or a life alone with only her books and characters to keep her company, but it would seem that would not be happening. She'd return home tomorrow and settle into the familiar routine of her family.

"Miss Marrington," the earl said from behind her.

She started at his voice and turned, hand to her chest. "You gave me a fright. You shouldn't sneak up on a person in such a way."

"Yes, well, I am not accustomed to knocking on doors in my own house."

He was a handsome devil, she'd give him that. Not terribly kind, though perhaps that was the way most people were here in town. The arrogance practically dripped from him, and exasperation lined his features, deepening his scowl

He stepped forward. "Incidentally, the door was open."

Yes, she had left it open after she'd returned from a light dinner downstairs. "Have you arranged for a carriage to return me home?"

"I would prefer you change your mind about leaving. Would you consider continuing with the assignment?"

Her heart stuttered at his words. He was asking her to stay? Perhaps this meant he was not as unreasonable as she'd first thought. "That depends on the situation here," she said.

"We are prepared to offer you more money," he said. His jawline ticked with tightening muscles. The stubble there drew her attention and she momentarily wondered if it would be rough or soft.

"I don't think you understand," she said. "There is not enough money to make this ordeal worth my trouble."

He nodded, took a deep breath. "Name your amount. I shall fund your dowry, if you need me to, and that of your unmarried sisters as well."

What was he talking about? She shook her head. "I am not asking for more money. I am only asking for you to treat me as an equal."

His brow furrowed. "We are not equals."

"Perhaps not by Societal standards, but for the purpose of this assignment, we are. You are the one who needs me."

"Yes, and I am offering you additional compensation."

"Is that how things work here in London?"

"I do not understand."

"Is this how all of London works, or is it only you who is so arrogant you do not consider the thoughts and feelings of others?"

She moved away from the window, came further into the middle of the room, and was aware of the fact that they were alone in a bedchamber. She stilled her nerves. "Do you merely toss money about to get people to do your bidding?"

His jaw twitched again, but this time she would have sworn that she saw a whisper of a smile.

"Is that amusing, my lord?"

"It is somewhat amusing that you managed to summarize the entirety of proper Society in one simple phrase. Yes, that is precisely how things work here in London. Money can buy you anything."

"Well, it cannot buy you a pretend queen."

"I don't think you're considering what a large sum of money could do for you," he said.

She knew what it could do for her. She could demand him purchase her a house and set her up with an allowance for life; that would ensure she be able to write and not be forced to marry. She longed for independence—from her family, the constraints on her gender, and most of all her mother's incessant badgering. It wouldn't be as bad if her mother even pretended to understand her middle daughter instead of continually trying to squeeze her into a mold that would not fit.

Oh, to have understanding and respect from her mother, but that would not happen; not because her mother didn't love her, she did, in her own way, but they were too different. So Evie relied on her own self-respect. Allowing the Earl of Somersby to continue to insult her and bark orders at her as if she were lower than a servant would equal walking away from that respect. Wasn't that the same thing as allowing her mother to force her into a marriage for money and prestige?

No, she could not do that and live with the treatment he'd give her. If he was a reasonable man, he could treat her better.

"I know what money can provide. I am not asking for

much, Lord Somersby. I want you to trust me, trust that when I say I can do this, I mean it. Trust that when I give you my word of confidence, that I will keep it no matter what."

"You do not know what you ask of me," he said, his words tight and firm.

Was her request so difficult?

"If I agree to these terms, you will stay and fulfill your duties to the assignment?" he asked.

She nodded. "Treat me as you would a man if you required such for this task. I can assure you, I am not a simpleton. I'm rather well-read. Perhaps my mannerisms are too country for the likes of royalty, but I can be taught. If I can learn Latin, I can learn to walk like the Queen." She was quiet a moment, then asked, "If you are so opposed to this charade, why are you the one they've asked to work with me? Certainly there are more men in your organization who could have taken your place."

"Indeed, Miss Marrington, indeed."

"Perhaps you could also apologize for the insults," she said.

His brows rose. "Insults?"

"I shall let it go, the things you said about my family, they are not a part of this. But the things you said about my person, I cannot work with someone who believes me to be an idiot." She waved her hand dismissively. "It matters not that you find me so unattractive, but I do not wish to be thought a fool."

He took a step closer to her. "You believe I find you unattractive?"

"You suggest otherwise? I'm fairly certain that any lady who is criticized for having wild and large hair and a pedestrian gait would make the same summary that I have.

As I said, that is inconsequential."

"I do not think you a simpleton." He inclined his head. "Anyone who can string the sentences together that you have today, calling out my actions and so forth. It is quite evident you are rather intelligent. It is apparent in your eyes." He glanced at the clock on the mantle. "We leave for Buckingham on the morrow. Perhaps we could continue this downstairs. Continue your instructions, that is."

So there was a gentleman inside of the Earl of Somersby. She found that realization both a relief and a concern, because someone so handsome could be dangerous were he also kind hearted.

"Do we have a bargain, Miss Marrington?" He held his hand out to her.

She eyed his offering, the large palm, his long fingers. She took his hand and it engulfed hers in a shake. "We have a bargain." Why did she feel as if she'd just irrevocably sealed her fate?

"For the record, I am not my family," she said once they had returned to his study.

There was such resolve in her features that he had no choice but to believe her, or at the very least to believe that she believed that. She was not her family. Obviously that meant she felt different in comparison.

Of course he'd seen the physical differences. Her sisters were all taller and more waif-like, not possessing Evelyn's sensual curves. Their features, too, were more subtle, none of them sharing her titian curls or shrewd blue eyes, but he suspected she did not mean those particular virtues when she spoke of her differences.

He could argue with her, show her precisely how attractive he found her, but that would only serve in terrifying the girl, and if her mother knew, he would most assuredly be heading for the altar. It was better that Evelyn believe he found her unappealing.

He nodded to her admission. "Shall we again work on the walking?"

She strode across the room and there was purpose in her movement, but still something seemed wrong about her posture.

"Try holding your head up and straighten your shoulders," he said.

Again she walked for him.

He shook his head.

"Show me?" she asked.

He stepped over and stood behind her, then put his hands on her waist. She stilled. He tried to ignore the gentle curve of her hips below his palms. He took one finger and slid it up the center of her spine. Her body responded and her shoulders straightened, her chin tilted up, and she sucked in a breath. Heat from her skin permeated through her dress, warming his fingers. Standing this close to her, he was surrounded by lavender and mint, scents utterly tantalizing and feminine. He resisted the urge to lean closer and inhale the coppery curls.

"Now, walk," he said. He followed along behind her, keeping his hand on her back. "Keep your shoulders straight. That's very good."

She turned and faced him and they stood that way, with

no words. Her lips parted and her wide eyes looked up at him.

He wanted to put his hands back on her waist, her back, anywhere. Damnation! What was the matter with him? "Perhaps we require a break." He rang for tea and they took seats in front of the hearth. Minutes later their tea service arrived and no sooner had they been served their cups that she began peppering him with questions.

"What other books have you read besides Frankenstein?" she asked.

He stirred his tea. "I don't get much reading time." Not completely the truth, he read quite often, but he was not interested in getting into a discussion that could lead back to Frankenstein.

"I suppose, as an earl, you're quite busy with the House of Lords." She bit into a sugared cake and flecks of sugar stuck to her lips. "What do you think about the new civil marriage act that Parliament recently passed?"

He tried not to stare at her mouth. "I have no opinion."

Her brow furrowed. "How can you have no opinion? Are you not a member of Parliament?"

"Technically, yes, I am, but I am not active. I am not political." He took a sip, hoping she'd follow suit, and the liquid would wash the infernal tempting sweetness off her pink lips. He'd expected this assignment to be tedious and boring, but not tempting.

She shook her head in confusion. "You work for the Crown. Is that not extremely political?"

"No, it has nothing to do with politics." His father had been a brilliant politician, but Bennett had never had the mind, nor patience for it. He served his country in other ways, notably by protecting. His brute strength had always been his greatest asset. "My duty is to the throne. I protect the throne, whomever sits upon it. I have no allegiance to them as a person, other than their birthright." He stood and went to the window. He glanced back at her. "You have sugar on your lips."

· · ·

She'd just had an entire conversation with the most beautiful man she'd ever seen and the whole time she'd had food on her mouth. How was she supposed to pretend to be the queen when she couldn't even go thirty minutes with an earl without embarrassing herself? She'd nearly swooned when he put his hands on her back. Obviously, she was too much of a goose; she would never be able to survive a real courtship. In truth, she was likely saving her mother a lifetime of embarrassment by refusing to entertain thoughts of marriage.

She tried to imagine how Jilly would handle this situation. Or Portia. No doubt they would have something clever to say to laugh off the faux pas. Of course, they would likely have never been in such a situation, as delicate and graceful as they were. As it was, Evie had allowed too much silence to pass between his comment and any would-be response. There was no clever response, simply mortification. She dared sneak a glance at him and thankfully he was still looking out the window.

"Is it raining?" she asked, finally breaking the silence.

Her turned back. "No, perhaps we shall have dry weather tomorrow when we move to Buckingham. I suppose we should go over that now. I need to familiarize you with the layout of the palace, the servants, and other persons you might encounter." He walked to the chairs near the hearth, his movements surprisingly elegant for a man his size.

"Yes!" she said, far too enthusiastically. She was relieved to have something for them to discuss. And for now, she'd stay away from the sugared cakes.

Chapter Five

They'd worked together at his townhome for a total of two days before heading to Buckingham Palace. Potterfield escorted them in only minutes before then disappeared into the tunnels beneath the palace to meet with the head council of the Brotherhood, which left Bennett and Evelyn alone in the Queen's private quarters.

Only time would tell whether or not Evelyn was ready, but Bennett felt certain she was as ready as any woman could be under the circumstances. She'd surprised him with her capableness and attitude. She was a hard worker and he could appreciate that.

So far her charade had been a success; none of the servants had even looked askew as he'd led Evelyn into the Queen's private chambers. He slid into her private chambers and closed the door behind. She looked up at his presence and came to her feet.

"This could be the last time we'll be alone together," he

said, walking towards her. Though that was likely untrue, he could hope. The less alone time they shared, the easier it would be for him to ignore his attraction to her. "We can't afford to compromise Victoria's reputation or yours."

She nodded.

"I've never been in here before," he said absently.

She scanned the room. "It's enormous, though I suppose that's not surprising. She is the queen. She likely has the best of everything." Her hand smoothed down the front of her gown. "This dress is magnificent, and the chemise is the finest of silks." Her eyes widened. She bit down on her lip.

He came to her, gripped her arms. "Nervous?"

She nodded and attempted to suck in a deep breath. "I don't normally discuss undergarments with gentlemen. My apologies, my lord."

"Remember, you cannot call me that here, and I care not about the propriety of such matters." Though he did care that he now had an image of her standing before him in nothing but her chemise. The fine silk hinting at the sensual curves of her flesh, her gorgeous titian hair billowing down her shoulders. He dropped his hands from her arms and stepped away.

Her amber eyes looked up at him and she shook her head. "I can't do this, I thought I could, but I can't. I can't fool all these people who know her." She shook her hands out in front of her. Her eyes filled with tears.

His stomach tightened and he wanted to pull her into his arms, hold her against his chest. He did not comfort women. Protect them, yes, but comfort them, never.

"All these people, servants, they'll all be watching my every move. I'm not accustomed to that."

He stepped closer to her, not close enough to touch her, but near enough he could see the uncertainty in her gaze. "It's one day, one event. People see what they want to see. They'll see the queen. We've given no one a reason to expect anything different." He inched forward, tipped her chin up so she would look at him. "Forget about the servants, forget about everyone but me. Can you do that?"

Her whiskey-colored eyes bore into his. "Yes."

"When you start to panic, find me in the room." He chuckled. "It is unlikely you'll be able to miss me as I'm normally the largest man in the room, but find me and know that all is well." He dropped his hand, but did not step away from her.

"What if you aren't there?"

"I'll be there." He was quiet a moment, and watched her. He wanted to reach for her hair, finger one of those vibrant red curls, but they bound her glorious mane and hid it beneath some manner of head covering. "Do you know the primary difference between you and Victoria?"

Her lips quirked in a grin. "Other than the fact that she's Queen of the Realm and I am the daughter of a country baron?"

"Yes, other than that." He didn't wait for her to answer. "It's nothing more than her confidence. She was raised to believe that she is worthy of being worshipped, worthy of fine gowns and jewels and the best of everything." He wanted to reach out and touch her, her arm, her face, something, instead he clinched his hands together in fists. "Think back to a moment when someone told you that you were beautiful, then think on that moment. It will give you more confidence."

Her brow furrowed. "I don't believe anyone has ever." She shook her head. "No one, well, save my father, has ever told me I was beautiful."

At that he could not resist reaching out and cupping her cheek. "You are beautiful, Evelyn Marrington. It's a pity no one has ever told you that." He hadn't wanted her to know; he'd worried his attraction would frighten her, but he could tell a woman she was beautiful without revealing how much he wanted her.

"My sisters are beautiful. I am…plain." Her head tilted. "Except for my hair, it is anything but. I seem to stand out in all the wrong ways."

"You are anything but plain."

The scent of her hair rinse wafted to him and his eyes fell to her lips, slightly parted, soft, pink. He wanted nothing more than to lean in the rest of the way and kiss her. She'd allow him to, she wanted it too; he could see it in her face. Hell, she'd already closed her eyes, and leaned in further.

• • •

He was going to kiss her.

Evie held her breath, closed her eyes, and waited for the first brush of his lips. Her heart fluttered and she wondered what she should do with her arms—put them up around his neck or put them at his waist—so she let them hang limply at her side. And then his hand was gone and he stepped away.

He cleared his throat. "You need to get your rest before tomorrow. I've arranged for a ladies' maid from my own staff to come and see to your needs. She is exceptionally loyal and will take care of anything you need."

"Of course. Thank you." Tears pricked at the back of her eyes. She wanted him to leave now. She'd practically thrown her arms around him and proclaimed herself a wanton. What had gotten into her? She never even flirted with men, let alone sought their kisses. And what had possibly made her think a man as dashing as Lord Somersby would even want to kiss her?

He walked to the door, turned and gave her once last glance. "Sleep well. I shall see you on the morrow."

She nodded, then exhaled loudly after he'd left the room. As if on cue, the ladies' maid entered to help her ready for bed. Normally, Evie would have spoken to the woman, but at the moment she was so close to tears she couldn't manage words. Not only that, but she was terrified she'd say the wrong thing, behave in a way that would reveal her charade.

She'd do well to remember that men like Lord Somersby did not go around kissing girls like her. He'd only been comforting her nerves, and he'd been attempting to convince her she was attractive. All part of his plan to ensure she stayed here to fulfill her duty to this task. She knew that he would do anything to make this assignment work, even tell her she was beautiful. Even nearly kissing her.

• • •

They'd waited until the rest of the opera goers had entered the theatre before Potterfield released Bennett and Evie from the carriage. Everyone would expect the Queen to be late. She would be able to enter without the prying eyes of people surrounding her. Once they were in her box, she'd have a few moments to compose herself before the onlookers realized the monarch had arrived.

Bennett led her to her seat. "When people begin to notice you've arrived, merely incline your head in recognition. It is unnecessary to wave."

She nodded, her eyes wide with fear.

"Breathe, you'll do great," he said.

She sat stone-still, staring blankly at the closed curtains of the stage below them.

"Relax," he said. Her posture was impeccable, he'd give her that, but she looked far better in this gown that the queen would. They were similar in stature, but Evelyn's curves were sinful, begging for glances, beckoning a caress. Damnation, he had to reign in these thoughts. He could not afford to lust after his assignment, especially since Potterfield had made it abundantly clear that either Bennett successfully complete this task or he'd be looking at doing nothing more than courier work for the Brotherhood.

"Precisely how am I supposed to accomplish that?" she asked through her teeth.

"We are at the opera, one of Her Majesty's favorite pastimes. You could at least pretend that you are enjoying yourself."

She glanced at him with those piercing amber eyes of hers.

The muscles across his abdomen tightened.

"I have never attended the opera before, but it's safe to say it hasn't actually started as of yet," she said. "What am I supposed to pretend to be enjoying?"

A grin tugged at his lips. "My company?"

She snorted with laughter, then covered her mouth with her fan.

"That wasn't intended to be a jest," he said. But her laugh had been genuine and had hummed across him in the most pleasant of ways. "It is true though. Victoria and I are cousins, and we are friends." And he'd never had any lustful thoughts about her. "People will expect us to be friendly with one another."

One brow arched. "Very well, perhaps if you could pretend to be charming, I could pretend to enjoy your company."

"Touché." He found himself smiling back at her.

"What do you and her normally discuss?"

"That is irrelevant. Any conversation I've had with her has already been had. It is our turn to converse."

She inclined her head. "Tell me of your family. Have you always lived in London?"

"No, my family's estate is in Berkshire, but my father was rather active with Parliament before he died so we spent much of our time here. Then when he died, my mother moved us here permanently."

"How old were you?"

"Fourteen."

"That's quite young to inherit an Earldom."

He shrugged. "It was what I was raised to do." Though his father had hoped Bennett would follow in his footsteps to make worthwhile changes in Parliament, Bennett had neither the desire nor the skill for such things.

"And you never wanted anything else?" she asked.

The types of skills that came natural to him weren't useful in the aristocracy, except for within the Brotherhood. There was never a reason to forcibly remove someone from a ball, but suspicious onlookers at coronation, he could take care of that. "I never entertained the idea of anything else. I knew I was heir." What did she want? Was it more than the life of a typical country miss?

"And your mother?"

"On husband number three," he said, and then immediately regretted it. He didn't need to share his private family stories with her, but it had noticeably eased her nerves. She was instantly more engaged with him, and onlookers were bound to notice. He wanted to tell her more, tell her how he loathed the way his mother seemed to parade her wares about looking for the next rich husband to take care of her, but he did not know her, nor was he in the habit of sharing his personal thoughts. It was an uncomfortable feeling. He shifted in his seat. It would have been easier had he rehashed a conversation he'd previously had with Victoria.

"Don't forget to, on occasion, look out at the crowd, give a pleasant smile, perhaps nod to a few," he said.

"Oh." She did what he suggested—looked out at the crowd, nodded and smiled pleasantly.

"I did not mean to speak out of turn, pry about your mother."

"You did not. I was already speaking of my family, it was a natural question."

She nodded. "Third husband?"

It angered him—if he were honest about it—that his mother had remarried so many times. His father had been a great man who had devoted his life to England and to the Crown. He'd spent all his life in service of the country. Yet after he'd passed, his mother had found one buffoon after another to entertain her, simply because she'd been bored, or more likely because she craved a certain luxurious lifestyle. It explained why all of her husbands had fat accounts.

"There's nothing to say about that. My mother does not like to be alone and she's a very handsome woman whom men seem fond of. Now then, tell me of your family."

She gave him a sly grin. "You met them."

"Yes, I did."

"They're big and loud, but lovely most of the time."

"Where do you fall in the line?"

"I am in the middle. Portia and Jillian are older, and Catherine and Meghan are younger. My sisters are all vivacious and beautiful and charming." Her words came out as if she'd said them before, or perhaps heard them repeated again and again. "I have always been my father's favorite though," she said with a grin.

"But you are not vivacious and beautiful or charming?"

She shook her head. "I am far too practical and too much in my own head, is what my mother says. 'Men don't care about your wild imaginings. They want to hear about themselves. If you cannot do that, simply talk about the weather.'" Then her eyes met his and her cheeks burned red.

"Your mother instructs you in these things?"

"Of course. She has made it her life's work to ready us for good matches and securing husbands."

He watched her then, noting the spark of intelligence in her eyes, the wittiness behind her grin. Her statement about her mother did not surprise him. He had seen the woman in action, but the fact that Evelyn herself admitted to being instructed to hunt and secure a good match, that did not fit with what he'd observed of her. Then again, had he not learned by experience that often it was the least assuming ones that turned out to be the most dangerous? "I see."

"Do you have siblings?"

"No."

"Are you married?" She cut her eyes at him, but her expression was unreadable.

"No." And then the curtain rose and the opera began. Perfect timing, as far as he was concerned. He was finished with that conversation.

Chapter Six

This would be the most delicate part of the evening — getting Evelyn out of the opera house and back to Buckingham.

People often lined up outside her box to catch a glimpse of the young queen. There would even be commoners outside on the street waiting for a peek at their monarch. Victoria might not be thriving in popularity right now, but she was a magnet for the curious. Bennett kept his hand at Evelyn's elbow.

Ellis and Adrian took the lead, and then Bennett moved Evelyn up the stairs out of her box and into the lobby of the theatre. The crowd was thick, ridiculously thick, all smiles and gawking in their direction.

It really was rather striking how much she favored Victoria, especially when her hair was bound and hidden beneath a larger than necessary crown and adorned with flowers. She nodded and smiled in response to the onlookers.

The smile transformed her face, and she no longer looked

like his royal cousin.

"Do not smile so broadly," he whispered to her. "Remember, nod ever so slightly to acknowledge them and then we move on. Do not stop walking."

She gave him a brief nod and tightened her grin. He hated to watch the spark in her eyes dim, but it was for her protection. Bennett used every inch of his looming height and kept his arms broad to prevent anyone from getting too close to her.

People called to her, some heckled, anything to get her to look in their direction. She nodded in their direction, but had no other reaction to the calls. In his periphery, Bennett could see several men standing with the crowd, men he knew, other members of the Brotherhood. Some of them had been assigned to mingle amidst the opera-goers, but others he was surprised to see. One in particular, though, seemed blatantly out of place. Phillip Wells, Earl of Morton; while a member of the Brotherhood, his only responsibility was to be the face of Potterfield's commands outside. Because of Potterfield's lower title, he couldn't expect higher-ranking aristocrats to follow his suggestions. Morton used his charm and handsome face to persuade people to follow the Brotherhood's wishes. But recently his erratic behavior caused Potterfield to nearly dismiss him. The man's membership, at this point, was a concession to the Queen's wishes.

The man in question squeezed his way through the crowd, came forward and very nearly got within touching distance of Evelyn. "My Queen," he said.

Evelyn looked at him and nodded politely, but Bennett kept moving her forward.

Adrian clipped Morton off, but the man looked at Evelyn,

studied her even, and Bennett could see it immediately that Morton knew this was not Victoria.

"We need to move," Bennett said, and Adrian and Ellis pushed past the rest of the crowd and out the doors to the bustling London street. Bennett blocked most of Evelyn's body with his own as they forced their way through the throng of people and into the waiting carriage.

Once they were safely ensconced in the carriage, Evelyn smiled excitedly. "I did it!" She exhaled loudly. "It was actually much easier than I anticipated, but you helped a lot."

Bennett swore.

"What's the matter?" Evelyn asked. "Did I do something wrong?"

"Someone recognized you."

• • •

Evelyn sat alone in her room for the first time in what seemed like weeks, even though she had been at Buckingham for two days. Her pencil poised above her paper, she tried to think of what else to do with her story. This was why she was here, wasn't it? To find inspiration to write her own adventure novels? But all she could think about was the night before.

Despite the fact that Bennett was convinced someone had recognized her, she had not seen anyone she knew. She deemed the evening a success. She had not tripped, nor made any large social mistakes. While she had not felt like a queen, she knew she must have looked like one because no one ever treated her so royally in her regular life.

Last night, she'd also gotten, what she realized, was a

rare glimpse into Lord Somersby. He was obviously not accustomed to speaking with people about such things, but they'd talked and he had been charming, and she'd nearly swallowed her teeth when he'd smiled at her. The grin transformed his face from the normal intensity to boyish good looks. Good heavens, if he wasn't the most attractive man she'd ever seen.

A footman broke her reverie when he knocked on the door and introduced a gentleman. She was not accustomed to the amount of servants the queen dealt with on a daily basis. She nearly stood, then remembered her place and kept her seat.

In walked a man that was beyond handsome. He was tall and slender and impeccably dressed with a stark white cravat, a rich emerald-green coat, and grey trousers. She knew by the way he moved, sleek and graceful, that he was confident, yet he did not seem to possess the gruff arrogance that Bennett had perfected.

The man's dark brown, almost black, hair created a sharp contrast to his pale and piercing blue eyes. When he smiled at her, his cheeks dimpled. He came forward, bowed deeply.

"I thought you might be getting lonely here so far away from your family." He grinned. "I am Philip Wells, Earl of Morton."

Panic rose in her throat. "So you know that I'm not…"

He leaned up against the desk, his foot swinging loosely, highlighting the sheen on his black boots. "Of course, my dear, I too am a member of the Brotherhood."

She relaxed some, tension tumbling off her shoulders. She was pleased to possibly have someone else to talk to, someone who knew she wasn't the Queen.

He moved closer to her, sat in a chair adjacent hers. "Tell

me, how are you enjoying your stay in London?" he asked, his voice smooth but low.

"It is rather pleasant, certainly more lively than life in the country, but as you're likely aware, my regular life is vastly different from this one." It was so welcoming to be able to talk about this with someone. Bennett didn't encourage discussion and hadn't asked her much of how she was managing things. The conversation they'd had the night before at the opera had been the most personal discussion between them. He'd even been charming.

"I myself have always preferred London. The country life is rather drab and boring for a fellow such as myself." He gave her a sly grin and a wink. "I admit that I enjoy the parties and clubs and the like far too much. Are you a card player?"

"No, I cannot say that I've ever developed much taste for any of the games." Of course that was generally because they were played in groups and she preferred more solitary activities.

"What is it that you do for pleasure?" he asked. He leaned in and again she was struck by how attractive he was; it was rather distracting. His eyes were alarmingly blue, and his grin so easy.

"I enjoy reading. Adventure novels, mostly, but I will read nearly anything."

He waved his hand dismissively. "I've never had the patience for reading. I'm afraid it made for a not so successful schooling." Again he winked. "I'd rather be out there living in the adventure than at home reading about it." He chuckled at his own jest. "But I suppose that's the benefit of being a man. Real adventure is far too dangerous for genteel ladies such as yourself."

"Indeed," she said, but beneath that she hid a retort that probably would irritate him. He'd been so pleasant and friendly thus far, it seemed a waste to annoy him and frighten him away, especially when he was only expressing an opinion that was widely held in their Society. She believed women could have adventures as well as any man, but she knew her opinion was an unpopular one. It was something she'd have to remedy in her own books.

Perhaps that was the problem. All of the books were written about the adventures that men had. She'd need to rethink her current idea, and give the adventure to the woman, though she had come to like her surly earl and the words that he spoke, so she couldn't cut him out of the book all together.

"If you do not enjoy games of chance, do you play any instruments or paint?" he asked.

"I play piano, though admittedly, I'm not very accomplished. I do enjoy music."

He crossed his leg over the other and nodded. "Ah, yes. How did you enjoy the opera last night? I found the Belgians to be a little melodramatic for my tastes."

Lord Morton certainly had his own opinions, and seemed none too reluctant to share them.

"I would have to agree with you, though I'm not certain my opinion would represent Her Majesty's."

His laugh rang through the large room. "Indeed. You are quite the charming woman, Miss—" Then he paused, a slight frown furrowed his brow. "I'm afraid I was not given your name."

"Evelyn Marrington." She nodded. "And thank you."

"Now then, you must tell me, how is Lord Somersby

treating you?"

Her heart stuttered at the mention of his name, an annoying affect. "He has taken great care with me and has instructed and assisted me every step of this journey." She tried to imagine Bennett and this man conversing, and the picture would not form in her mind. "Are you and he friends?"

A cross expression came to Lord Morton's face. "Perhaps we could have been at some point, but I'm afraid I do not hold the man in high esteem. I shall not speak ill of him though since he is a champion to you."

Curiosity shot through her. She was not one to gossip, but in truth she knew very little about Bennett, and she could not deny he was quite intriguing. "Oh, no, he is merely my guide here. I could not say that I truly know him at all."

He learned further over. "I probably should refrain from telling you this, but since it is all truth, then it can't constitute as gossip. You see, he was engaged to be married once upon a time to a beautiful woman who gave him her heart."

The beautiful woman who had come to his townhome, that had to be her. Evie had noted that they had a past. "Go on," she said.

"Somersby tired of her, leaving her destitute at the altar. Her reputation was shattered, no one would have married her or even allowed her to govern their children." He shook his head, his features spoke of concern and pity. "I did the noble thing and married her since Lord Somersby walked away. It was the only solution."

She'd heard something similar at that first ball when Bennett had walked in, that he'd jilted some poor woman. At the time she'd assumed it was idle gossip, not at all the kind of thing she'd lend credence to. Now that she knew Bennett better she didn't know what to think. She would have sworn he was incapable of such dishonor, but how well did she truly know him? A few days in a man's company was not enough to know his character, and he certainly hadn't treated her very well when they'd first began this journey. "That was quite generous of you," she said.

"Unfortunately, I believe no one in the Brotherhood has ever forgiven me for making Somersby look bad. None of Somersby's cohorts treat me with the same respect I provide them." He gave her a smile. "But as I said, I have not had a good experience with the man, though it does not mean that he is all bad."

She didn't believe him all bad. She wasn't even sure he was bad at all. And then as if she's summoned him merely from thought, he walked into the room. He saw her first, and then his eyes landed on her companion and Bennett's frown turned into a glower. The muscles along his jawline clenched and his fists knotted at his sides. He strode directly to Lord Morton.

"Out," he said, though he did not yell. The intensity in that one word skittered chills across the back of her neck.

The man stood. "I believe I have been dismissed. It has been my pleasure, Miss Marrington." He bowed to her. "I do hope we can see one another soon."

Her pulse raced and she could scarcely take her eyes off Bennett. If she'd needed a reminder of how much she did not know the man, here it was, in a huge hulking pile of anger. "Yes, thank you," she said to Lord Morton.

Bennett slammed the door after both men had left the room.

Perhaps Lord Morton had spoken the truth—Bennett was arrogant and rude. He couldn't simply storm in there and demand her guest leave! Well, she presumed he could do that considering this was not her palace and he was likely trying to protect her. Still, it would seem that another member of the Brotherhood would be a perfectly safe visitor for her to have. There was obviously more to the relationship between Lords Morton and Somersby. She intended to uncover precisely what that was.

. . .

It was all Bennett could do not to slam Morton's perfectly dressed body against the wall and then pound his fist into the man's perfect face. "What the devil do you think you're doing here?" Bennett asked once they were in the corridor.

"Do you believe me a fool, Somersby?" The arrogance in Morton's stance and expression made it doubly difficult not to punch him. "I knew as soon as I saw her last night that she wasn't the queen. Where is Victoria?"

"That is not any of your concern." Bennett did his best to keep his tone even. Yelling would solve nothing. "And you can wipe that snide look off your face, Morton."

He had the audacity to appear surprised at that. "This is official work of the Brotherhood. Need I remind you that I am still a member of the order? That Her Majesty, herself, insisted I be retained?"

Bennett moved his hand close to Morton's throat simply to watch the fear shudder across his pretty face, then he straightened the man's cravat. "No, you need not remind me about anything." Two months earlier the Brotherhood had voted to remove Morton from their membership, but the queen stepped in and demanded he be allowed to remain.

Victoria had a soft spot for the Earl of Morton. Bennett suspected it was the same with all women, enchanted by the man's handsome features. No wonder Gwyneth had chosen him over Bennett. He was prettier than some of the women in London. More than likely he took as long as a lady to ready himself for the day.

"I came to introduce myself to the young woman. No doubt you have been as surly with her as you are with everyone else." He tugged on his waistcoat. "And your obscene size must frighten the poor girl."

Bennett did not take the bait.

"I came to demand answers."

Bennett laughed. "You are in no position to demand any-thing. Potterfield followed Her Majesty's wishes and retained you as a member, but it is in name only. You are privy to no information."

"The devil I'm not." Morton made the mistake a stepping towards Bennett. "I shall go straight to Her Majesty and tell her all about this nonsense."

Bennett allowed himself to loom at his full height over the shorter, thinner man. "Go ahead, do it. See if you can find her."

"You cannot do this."

Bennett half expected the man to stomp his foot as a child would.

"I shall get the answers I want one way or another, or I'll— "

Bennett took a step even closer to the man. "Or you'll what?"

"I'll go forward to *The Times*. I'll tell them that the

woman living in Buckingham is a fraud, that something dreadful has happened to the Queen, and that you are responsible."

Bennett schooled his features. He would report this to Potterfield later, but for the moment, there was no reason to take the threat with any seriousness. "Who do you suppose will believe you? You are dreadfully close to being sent to debtor's prison, despite Her Majesty's obvious lack of insight when it comes to you. No one else in this town would pay you any heed. And when that time comes, Victoria won't be there to save you. She might have stepped in the last time, but only because she doesn't know the entire truth about you."

"We shall see about that. Women always believe me, they trust me. Why right now, that girl in there is thinking about the wretched thing you did to poor Gwyneth."

Bennett seethed. He grabbed Morton by the throat and slammed him into the wall.

"Somersby!" Potterfield called from behind them. "Let him go."

"He has threatened the Brotherhood. Infiltrated Her Majesty's private offices to seek an audience with her," Bennett said, not moving his hand from Morton.

The handsome man's eyes watered and his hand turned red as he clawed at Bennett's vice-like grip.

"Let him go," Potterfield said again. "Now."

Bennett did as he was told.

Morton gasped for air and put his hand to his throat. "You are a monster," he whispered hoarsely.

Bennett made to walk off and Potterfield put a hand to his arm. "We will discuss this later."

Bennett had never liked Phillip Wells. He'd always seen him as an inflated pompous ass, but today when he'd found him sitting with Evelyn, it had gone past irritation or dislike. He'd been ready to throttle the man. His reaction had been completely irrational. Perhaps he was angry because he knew Mortan had recognized that Evie wasn't the queen. That was the only explanation that made sense. Her safety in Buckingham could be at stake and Victoria's reputation could be in even more danger.

And he'd told her about Gwyneth, which meant he'd told her the version of the story he always told, that Bennett had jilted her and he swooped in and rescued her reputation. Morton always conveniently left out the part of when Bennett had found Morton and Gwyneth together in bed. His own bed, no less. He'd come home early from an assignment and he'd ended their relationship that night, kicked them both out of his house. But if Bennett knew anything about Morton it was that the man was ridiculously lazy and unmotivated. It was primarily what made him an ineffective member of the Brotherhood, that and the fact that Bennett had always believed the man had a price. People who could be bought or persuaded by any sum of funds were dangerous.

Now it was time to deal with Evelyn. Bennett took several deep breaths before he entered the room where he'd left her. There was no reason to be angry with her; she hadn't done anything wrong. Unless she'd told that bastard something. The calming breaths forgotten, he opened the door and glowered in her direction.

"You are surly," she said as he stepped into the room.

It was evident she'd been pacing the length of the room

as she'd stopped midstride to speak to him.

"It's as if no one ever taught you to smile," she said.

"What?"

"Lord Morton said that of you and he's absolutely correct, you are constantly surly. You've been scowling since I met you. In fact…" She held up one finger. "The only time I've ever seen you smile is last night at the opera, and I believe that was an act to fool the onlookers."

Bennett's hands clenched. "Yes, well, we all can't afford to be as charming as Lord Morton."

She rolled her eyes and gave a little shake of her head. "Well, that is a ridiculous sentiment. It takes no extra time to be charming, only effort."

"I cannot believe you granted him an audience. Did you not hear me last night when I told you that someone recognized you?"

"You said precisely that." She pointed at him, her frown heavy on her brow. "Someone recognized me, but I saw no one I knew."

"I meant that someone realized you were not the queen."

"That is a vastly different statement."

"With the same result," he yelled back, then instantly regretted it. If he frightened her, she'd likely run back to Essex. Then again, her staying likely no longer mattered. Yes, they had decided to use her for an additional appearance, the reason he'd come to see her, but Potterfield had seen him lose his temper with Morton and Bennett would pay for that. Perhaps the ultimate price, his future with the Brotherhood.

"How was I supposed to know that?" She shook her head, exasperation vibrating off her. She certainly did not seem the least bit frightened by his outburst. "Besides," she said, "he never pretended to believe I was Victoria. He came in and introduced himself as a member of your Brotherhood. Is that not true?"

Bennett exhaled slowly. "Technically, that is true, but not every member is privy to all details. Only a handful who know you are here."

"Still, he was very friendly and charming, and he seemed far more concerned with how I'm doing with all of this. You haven't asked me even how I'm feeling, other than to ensure I'm going to follow through with the assignment."

Her cheeks flushed when she was angry and it made him wonder what she'd look like in the throes of passion. That was one of the reasons why he didn't inquire to her well-being. He didn't want to spend any more time with her than was necessary, because being in her presence made him want to toss her onto the bed and run his fingers through her fiery red hair. He shoved the desires aside.

"What did you discuss with him?" Bennett asked as he crossed the room. He loomed over her, fully acknowledging that his size alone could intimidate or frighten her, he'd been able to utilize that to his benefit since the summer he turned sixteen, but thus far she seemed unflappable..

She stood straight, her petite height only bringing her to his chest, but did not cower. "I don't see how that is any of your business. My discussions on my own time should not be relevant."

Though her words annoyed him, the fact that she did not seem the least bit intimidated by him, inexplicably pleased him. "Perhaps if you were on your own time, but you are currently in my employment and thus your private conversations are very much my concern."

"If you think because you are larger than me that you can intimidate or frighten me, you are sadly mistaken." She poked one finger into his chest and looked up at him through narrowed eyes.

He reached out to pull her to him. He wanted to kiss her so badly it made him step backwards. "He told you about Gwyneth, did he not?"

Surprise softened her features. "He did."

He nodded.

"Do you want to know what he told me, specifically?" she asked.

"I'm certain I can deduce what the man said." He wanted to defend himself, tell her the truth about what had happened, but none of it mattered, least of all her opinion of him. She was merely an assignment, though he knew that wasn't entirely the truth. "There are always other sides of a story," he added in spite of himself.

"She is the reason you remain unmarried?"

He nodded.

"But you shall marry someday, will you not?"

"To produce an heir. It is my responsibility to not allow my title to die with me."

She frowned. "You make it sound so formal. What of love and affection?"

"Love is nothing more than an illusion. Marriage is a business decision."

"That is not true. I've seen love between married couples."

"You've seen what people want you to see. Nothing more." He was done with this conversation. Debating the merits of love was a futile exercise. "That was all that was discussed?"

"If you want to know if I told him anything that you have spoken to me in confidence, then I did not," she said. "I believe I told you once that I am trustworthy. If you don't believe me, then you shouldn't have brought me here."

"I didn't have a choice in the matter."

"What is that supposed to mean?"

"Precisely what I said. You, this—" He spread his arms out to encompass the room. "Is an assignment, and not one I asked for."

Pain flickered across her eyes, but she took a breath, lifted her chin a notch. "My apologies for inconveniencing you so."

"That's not what I said." There it was, still that desire to lower his lips to hers. He walked to the other side of the room and picked up a book as if that was what he'd intended to do.

"When do I return home?" she asked.

That surprised him. She hadn't backed down from a fight yet, but now she was ready to leave. Of course, who could blame her, he'd been a complete ass to her today. "Not yet. I know we said the opera would be it and then you could leave for your family's cottage, but it would seem we need you a while longer. That is what I was coming to tell you."

"What of—"

He held a hand up. "You will be compensated for the additional days." Women and their incessant need for money. "Tomorrow afternoon they are laying the beginning of the railroad track that will ultimately lead from London to Brighton. The railway engineer will be there to explain the route, as well as a few other officials. You do not need to say anything, but it will be good for public opinion for Her

Majesty to be seen supporting industrial advancement."

"I see." Whatever fire he'd lit in her this evening with his accusations and temper, he'd successfully cooled. Her clipped tone chilled him, that and perhaps she had believed the story Morton told her. She hadn't asked him about it, hadn't asked him to deny the accusations. It was for the best if she believed the worst of him. He was here to protect her, not seduce her.

"I will be here in the morning to brief you on the situation," he said. "Fortunately, these are not people Victoria already knows so you won't have to pretend to remember them."

She nodded.

Damnation, he should not be annoyed that she wasn't fighting him, yet he was. She was being ridiculously compliant. "You are not having second thoughts, are you?"

"No, of course not."

But he wasn't completely assured by her response, nor was he reassured by the fact that he was too involved in her emotions, in her, if he were honest. Normally his work called for him to show up, use his instincts to protect the Queen, then go home. But with Evie everything was becoming increasingly complicated, and that made him nervous.

Chapter Seven

Stand and wave.

Stand and wave.

That was all she needed to do. Oh, and not forget to breathe, and appear as if she were the Queen of England. Shouldn't be too difficult. She'd survived the opera the other night without even a hitch. Granted, there she had spent the majority of the time in a theatre box far removed from the people.

This need not be any different. Still, her nerves were on fire. She took a deep breath, in and out. This was so different from her regular life, posing as the Queen aside. At home she so easily hid in the middle of her sisters, effectively staying out of the center of attention, but here, there was no hiding. Everyone looked at her, everyone acknowledged her. Was this how it felt when Jilly walked into a ballroom? To have every male head turn with appreciation and every female wince with just a little envy? Surprisingly enough, Evie couldn't deny that while the attention was overwhelming, there was part of her that enjoyed it. Female vanity; she would never had guessed she possessed any. Her mother would be so proud.

Bennett stood at her side as they waited for the rest of the men who would escort her to the platform. Between them, Bennett reached over and barely brushed his fingers against hers, though he did not grab her hand. Her breath caught. She did not dare glance at him, but knowing he was right here next to her soothed her. The warmth of his hands permeated the fine silk of her gloves, and she wished in that moment they were somewhere else, perhaps different people, so she could grab his hand and link their fingers.

"You'll do fine," he said.

And then she was being led from the carriage up to the platform. It was the starting of a train depot, but at the moment consisted mostly of a framed building and a stage-like area. Freshly laid tracks gleamed in the sunlight.

The man at the podium acknowledged her, thanked her for coming, then went about explaining the design and route that the railway would take from her to Brighton. She inclined her head and gave what she hoped was a regal wave, then he continued talking.

She scanned the area, searching for a friendly face, but found none. From here, the crowd all looked the same. The poor to one side, the rich to the other, instinctively separating themselves as they would be on the train, as they were in town.

Behind her right shoulder stood Bennett. Without turning around, she could see him in her periphery. His stern features were set in a fierce glare as he watched the people around her. He was not far, but not so close he could touch her.

"Does Her Majesty wish to address the crowd?" the man at the podium asked.

It took a moment for his words to register with her, and she was formulating a response when Bennett stepped forward and whispered something to the man. He nodded and smiled brightly at Evelyn.

"Our gracious Queen does not wish to take any focus off the railway today," the man said.

The crowd cheered; well, some of them did, perhaps even most of them, but a few snickered and jeered. Though she could not see where the naysayers stood, she heard their voices loud above the applause of the others. Bennett had mentioned something about Victoria not being popular with much of England, but seeing that in action was jarring.

Still Evie smiled, and inclined her head in a slight bow. The man got everyone quieted and then continued to drone on about the railway construction. Evie had never given much thought to England's monarch, but in this moment, she felt an enormous amount of sympathy for her Queen. Not only did the woman have to endure such events, but she had to do so while weather jeers.

She looked out at their faces, wondering what it was that made them hate her so. Then she saw him, a figure in the crowd moving effortlessly toward the stage.

• • •

Bennett watched the crowd, looking for anything out of the ordinary. He glanced back at Evie as the man at the podium continued to talk about the amazing attributes to the upcoming railroad. She, too, looked out at the crowd. People called to her, some cheered, some yelled spiteful things, cruel words that neither Evie nor Victoria deserved.

Then in a flash, she was laid out on the platform, a man on top of her. People screamed. Bennett picked up the man and tossed him off the platform, then scooped up Evie's body and raced to the carriage.

"Are you hurt?" Bennett asked, again and again.

Evie looked up at his face, but didn't answer.

"I need you to tell me if you're hurt," he said.

She concentrated on his face. "What?" She shook her head. "No, I don't believe so, merely startled."

He tucked her into the carriage, and climbed in beside her. "I shall check everything out when we get back to the palace."

She shook her head, wrapped her arms around her middle. "That won't be necessary." Fear widened her eyes. "What was the man trying to do?"

Bennett said nothing, only clenched his jaw. He pulled back the small curtain on the carriage and stared outside. The ride back to Buckingham went by in silence. When he'd seen her go down, fear sliced through him. But he'd gotten the man off before he'd killed her, though he'd obviously injured her. With every bump and bounce of the carriage, she winced, though she did her best to put on a brave face.

Finally the carriage rolled to a stop and he once again grabbed her. This time he took her hand rather than carried her into the palace. He led her up the stairs and then into a room at the end of the corridor.

"What is this room?" she asked.

"It is where the Privy Council meets." He led her directly to the fireplace and pushed down on a small statue. There was a click and then the fireplace shifted, revealing a hidden staircase.

Her breath caught. "Wow," she whispered.

He led her down, then moved a lever on the wall and the passage behind them closed. He said nothing, but continued moving forward until they'd reached an antechamber. He went about lighting the wall sconce lanterns, then turned to face her.

"Now then, where are you hurt? And don't bother telling me that you aren't, I've seen you wince."

"I told you, I am fine." But her body betrayed her with a jab of pain on her side. She grabbed onto it, her eyes falling shut. "I can inspect it myself. I need to get to my bedchamber."

His brow furrowed. "Where?"

She released a hiss of a breath. "You are so stubborn. Here." She touched her left side and winced at the feel of her own fingers.

"I need to see it."

"You can't see it, it is beneath my clothing."

He nodded and the realization fell onto her. Her mouth opened in a silent "o."

"It is purely a medical examination," he said, unsure if he was trying to convince her or himself, but right now his concern for her wellbeing outweighed his lustful thoughts about seeing her without her clothes.

"Certainly there is someone more appropriate to examine me. Do you even have medical skills?"

"Some," he said. "We cannot afford to allow anyone see you, or rather Victoria, in this state. I need to assess the situation before I bring the information to the others, see if we need to risk calling in a physician."

"Here, you can examine me this way." She moved closer to him, held her arms up out of the way so he could reach her side.

"I need to see it, Evelyn." He swore. "Either you take that dress off or I'll take it off for you."

Her heart pounded and her mouth went dry. "You will have to take it off for me, as I cannot reach all of the fastenings. I still think this is completely unnecessary." She turned her back to him so he could have access to her buttons.

He swore again. His warm breath skittered across her skin.

"What is the matter with you? I am the one that was hurt."

"Precisely. This is a situation that should never have happened. We shouldn't have brought you here to London, should only have cancelled the events," he said, all the while working on her buttons. "Told everyone that the Queen had a bit of an injury and waited for her to recover."

A cool draft brushed against the back of her neck as her dress fell open. It still left her corset and chemise in place that he'd have to remove.

"I should not have had to save you."

"I will not apologize because I did nothing wrong," she said sharply. It seemed entirely ridiculous that he was angry with her for something that was not her fault.

He was quiet and still for several moments. "Is that what you think?" he asked, his voice quiet, almost gentle. "That I am angry with you for this?"

She tried to glance at him over his shoulder. "Obviously you are."

"No." He traced a finger against the bare skin of her

back. "I am angry with myself for not protecting you."

"Oh." Her body was riding a war of sensations; pleasure from his touch and pain from her side. She'd take the pain if he'd touch her again.

He pushed the dress off her shoulders, then began working on loosening her corset. "You're bleeding."

She tried to see the injury, but she could not see anything. "Where?"

"Right here." His finger brushed gently against her side. "Doesn't appear to be too much blood, but I need to see the injury." He tugged and pulled on the corset until he'd released it and lifted it off her.

Then it was her shift, which he was able to pull up, rather than remove. "It looks as though he cut you, a knife or some sort of blade. It's not very deep though." His touch was gentle as he explored the area at her side.

The injury hurt, she couldn't deny that, but that was not the sensation that she focused so intently on. His fingers rubbing lightly against her bare flesh sent shivers through her. She had only ever been in this state of undress with maids and her sisters, never a man. Anytime she was the least bit embarrassed, an ugly stain of red blotched her skin. She must be positively covered in it at the moment, but she shoved the thought aside. It wasn't as if Bennett would find her appealing in any circumstance.

"Evelyn, I think you'll be all right." His hand cupped the dip at her waist. "I'm going to need to clean this wound and bandage you."

"Do you have everything you need down here?" She glanced around the antechamber, noting the carved out stone walls.

"Yes, I have what I need."

Then she frowned. "Where are we?"

"Below the palace."

· · ·

Bennett moved to a cabinet and opened it, searched through it. Once these tunnels had been completed, the Brotherhood made certain that these rooms were well-stocked with anything they might need, everything from wine to dried fruits and medical supplies, anything that might be necessary in an emergency. He found what he needed—bandages, a basin, and a jug of water. There were also supplies for sutures if they were required, but he hoped it wouldn't come to that.

Footsteps sounded down the tunnels. He had expected others to come and check on her well being. Potterfield was the first to round the corner into the room, but he stopped short when he saw Evelyn's state of undress.

"Beg your pardon," he said, and stepped back around the corner.

Bennett moved back to her, tried his best to ignore the sight of her bare back splayed before him, but damned if the sight of her fair skin didn't have blood surging to his groin, despite the fact that her injury still bled. Thankfully it had slowed, a good sign that she was not injured too badly, but there was always the concern for infection.

"Is it a serious injury?" Potterfield asked loudly enough for them to hear.

"This is mortifying," Evie murmured.

"Haven't cleaned it yet," Bennett said. "But it doesn't look too bad thus far."

He poured some water into the basin and carried it over to her. Damnation, this was a situation neither of them should have been in, but her especially. She was a bloody country miss, not some war-trained woman tested in the art of battle.

"That man should never have gotten near the platform," Bennett said to Potterfield. "Why didn't the men in the crowd catch him? You did have men down there, did you not?"

"Of course," Potterfield said. "I spoke to the guards we had on the ground. They all said he looked unassuming, that they didn't even notice him until he was right there at the platform. And who would have guessed he could have jumped onto the platform? When I agreed to Her Majesty attending, I was given the measurements of the platform."

"Obviously they were wrong," Bennett said.

"I saw him coming," she said quietly. "I didn't realize truly what I was seeing, but he was coming right at me."

"If others come down here," he said to Potterfield, "keep them out of the room until I'm finished with this." Bennett dipped the rag into the water. "This might burn." He proceeded to clean the wound.

She winced, but said nothing.

"I'm sorry if you were frightened," he said low enough that only she would be able to hear. He kept his attention to the task at hand, refusing to notice how deliciously pale and creamy her skin was compared to his, or the way the muscles in her side tensed and tightened as he cleaned.

"That man," she said, her voice shattering his thoughts. "He intended to kill me, her, the Queen."

"Yes." Finally he'd cleaned the wound enough to see that it was little more than a graze of whatever kind of blade he'd used. Had she not being wearing all the layers of clothing, it would have done more damage. "Knife wound," he told Potterfield. "Not too deep though."

"We'll need to watch for infection," Potterfield said. "There is some salve—"

"Already have it out," Bennett said. He wanted Potterfield to leave, to get the hell out of there, not merely because then he'd be alone with Evie, but because right now that was who Bennett blamed for the incident. "Had you not demanded we bring her to London for this charade, none of this would have happened."

"Not true. This would have happened to Her Majesty. Precisely where are your loyalties, Somersby?" Potterfield asked.

Bennett swore under his breath.

"And the people in the crowd who sneered at me," Evie said. "Why? Why do people hate her so?"

"Some don't want her to be queen. They believe her too young, too inexperienced." He smeared some salve on the cut, then proceeded to bandage her. "You were fortunate. I believe your corset saved you."

"Thankfully I was wearing one of Her Majesty's corsets and not one of my own, as mine are far less sturdy than hers, the fabric much thinner."

"That should do it, but it will likely still pain you for the next few days. When we get to your room, I suggest you have a nice swallow of brandy to ease the pain."

"I shall endure."

Bennett pulled her dress back up over her corset. "We need to get you dressed and back into your rooms before rumors start that the queen has been abducted or killed."

She turned to face him, grabbed his hand. "Thank you for saving me."

He nodded but said nothing. He should be thankful that it had been Evelyn who had been injured and not the Queen, but he wasn't. And therein lay the problem. What was so different about this woman that he'd allowed her to get to him? His sole purpose was to protect the monarch, whoever that might be. Yet, that was not what he thought of when he'd seen her go down on the platform. He'd jumped into action, but he'd been afraid for her. And that concerned him more than any potential threat to the Queen.

Chapter Eight

Bennett left Evelyn and immediately went back into the Brotherhood tunnels to discuss matters with Potterfield. He'd be damned if he'd allow Evie to continue to be placed in such danger. She had not signed up for that and she could have been killed today. This had quite obviously gone too far.

It took him a while to locate them, but he found precisely who he'd been looking for. Potterfield sat in one of the rooms speaking with Adrian and Ellis.

Potterfield looked up and saw him and nodded. "How is Miss Marrington fairing?"

Ellis came to his feet, concern lining his features.

Bennett ignored Evelyn's cousin and did his best to reign in his anger as he faced Potterfield. "How is she fairing?" Bennett said through clenched teeth. He made his way over to the table and braced his hands on it, leaned forward. "Have you lost your senses? She is an innocent country miss and today she was attacked." He pounded a fist on the table. "With a knife. She's cut, bleeding, and we can only pray that infection and fever don't set in."

"Did you clean the wound?" Adrian asked.

Bennett glared at Adrian. "Of course I did. I'm not a damned idiot!"

"There is no reason to lose your temper in here, Somersby. Sit down where we can discuss this as reasonable people," Potterfield said.

Bennett ignored his command and continued to stand.

Ellis swore, sat back down. "I should never have suggested her."

"No, you shouldn't have," Bennett said. "I want her taken back home. Now. She's done her part. Give her the money you owe her and then I will bring her home."

Potterfield shook his head. "We cannot do that yet."

"Why the hell not?" Bennett asked.

"I heard from Lynford today. The Queen has not recovered from her previous injury. Her ankle has not healed and she's hobbling around on it." Potterfield eyed Bennett. "We cannot afford to send Miss Marrington home right now."

Bennett pushed his fingers through his hair and swore. "This has gotten out of control. She's not trained for this sort of task."

"Then train her," Potterfield said simply.

"Must I remind you that we do not have women in the Brotherhood?" Why was he the only one concerned about Evelyn's safety? Every member of the Brotherhood, at least those on the upper tier who did the actual protecting, would lay their life down for their monarch, but it was wrong for them to assume or expect that from the daughter of a baron.

"True, but there have been women in every other agency that the government has used," Potterfield said. "Our spies, our monarchs. Is she incapable in some way?"

"No, she's not incapable. But she is a woman," Bennett said. Damnation! He didn't know if he was angrier with himself that she'd gotten injured on his watch, or with Potterfield for putting this charade together.

Ellis had started pacing. "We cannot get my cousin killed. My aunt would never forgive me."

"Then it is settled. You must train her," Potterfield said. "Teach her whatever it is that you think she needs to know to survive."

"So, you are suggesting that I teach her hand-to-hand combat? And what is next? Shall I teach her how to fire a weapon? How to knock a man out with her parasol? How to gut a man with a dagger?"

"If those are the skills you believe she needs, then yes. You certainly should. Are you not always reminding us that women are stronger than they look? That they're as capable as men?"

"Am I to do the same for Victoria when she returns?" Bennett said, ignoring Potterfield's questions. Yes, he often told the men of the Brotherhood that they should not be so fooled into thinking that women were weak and helpless. Those affects were merely another way women manipulated men. "I believe I've suggested as much before."

Potterfield looked at the other men, then frowned. "So you have. It is definitely something we need to discuss. Historically, the Brotherhood has always trained the monarchs in some defense skills, but it was not even something we considered when Victoria was crowned."

"I believe someone said she was the pinnacle of genteel propriety and to teach her how to wield any weapon would be a disgrace," Bennett said.

"She is a lady, but also our monarch. If our law allows women to be the monarch, then our practices should be the same regardless of king or queen," Potterfield said. "Beginning tomorrow, you teach Miss Marrington whatever you think she needs."

Potterfield never took Bennett's suggestions. It seemed ridiculous that this was the one that would finally move forward. "What she needs is to be safely back at home."

Potterfield leveled his gaze on Bennett. "If you are unwilling to do this, Somersby, I am certain that I can find someone who is."

"I shall do it," Adrian said, coming to his feet.

Potterfield held his hand out, indicating he was quite ready to hand Evie over to someone else.

On one hand, Bennett would like to pass off the duties to show that he didn't agree with this situation, but he knew that if he walked away now, he might as well keep walking because his time with the Brotherhood would be over. Not only that, he wasn't certain he trusted anyone else to ensure Evie's safety, especially Adrian. He was a notorious rake.

"You are practically suggesting I make her a full member of the Brotherhood." Bennett raked his fingers through his hair. "How can you be so flippant about this? It is her life we are talking about, her safety."

"Gentlemen," Potterfield said, directing his attention to Ellis and Adrian. "I should like a moment alone with Lord Somersby, please."

The other two men stood and left the room, their steps

echoed down the stone tunnel.

"Our allegiance, in case you have forgotten, is to the crown, and right now that is Her Majesty, Queen Victoria," Potterfield said. "This girl is nothing more than a servant doing a task. She is disposable, if necessary."

Bennett wanted to hit him, but he held his temper in check.

"She could have been killed."

"Better her than the queen," Potterfield said plainly.

He should agree, he knew he should, but damned if that felt wrong. When he'd seen Evie go down beneath that man, he'd been ready to rip the man from limb to limb to protect her. Would he feel the same had it been Victoria on that platform? Certainly he would.

The man's brows rose slowly. "If you have developed some sort of attachment to the girl—"

"No, I have not. She is an assignment." But even as he said the words, doubt gnawed at him. "She is a civilian, Potterfield. Can we ask her to make the ultimate sacrifice?"

"Did you not tell her there were risks to this assignment?"

Had he? He couldn't remember. He'd been so angry about being forced to work with her, he likely hadn't properly prepared her.

"Sit down," Potterfield said, his words even. "We have other matters to discuss."

Bennett released a heavy breath and fell into one of the chairs.

"You cost us that man today."

That he hadn't been expecting. "I beg your pardon. I believe I did my job and saved Her Majesty."

"You tossed the man off the platform and into the

crowd." Potterfield shook his head. "We lost him. He got away, and now he's still out there and could potentially come after her again."

"I saved her," he said again.

"You reacted in anger, just as you did to Morton the other day outside of the Queen's rooms."

"Morton is a bastard."

"Be that as it may, you cannot simply go about putting your hands on people in such a way. You must learn to control yourself. Damnation, Bennett, you're more intelligent than this. You do not need to use your strength to overpower every situation. But if you continue to do so, there will be no future for you in the Brotherhood. We risk too much by your actions."

. . .

Evie stepped into the tunnels exactly as she had done earlier with Bennett. She could hear them arguing down the corridor, Bennett and someone else, another man. She inched closer to better hear their voices. The tunnel was dimly lit so she put her hand to the carved stone wall and followed it forward. Her fingertips chilled beneath the cold rock. She heard her cousin's voice up ahead.

"We shall cancel it, give some excuse as to why the queen won't attend," Ellis said. "No one will question it."

"They will," another man said. "Already the country is at odds, people believe her to be too young to effectively lead. Any show of weakness right now could destroy her chance at becoming a worthwhile monarch."

"Well, I don't want to put Evelyn in any additional

danger," Ellis said. "I should never have suggested this. It's too risky."

Where was Bennett in all of this? Light flickered ahead and she turned right down the tunnel.

"If Somersby is so reluctant to complete this assignment, then he should step aside and allow someone else to do it."

Bennett was reluctant to continue working with her? Disappointment fell heavy onto her.

"If he can't or is unwilling to ready the girl for the event, I shall do it," the man said.

She'd heard enough. She followed the tunnel to where they stood discussing her as if she had no opinion in the matter. "I don't see any reason why you have to hide down here and discuss me." It was Ellis and another gentlemen, whom she'd seen the night of the opera, though she had not been formally introduced.

Bennett chose that moment to step out of one of the rooms. His gaze fell on her and his frown deepened. "Evelyn," Bennett said. "What are you doing down here?" He moved forward to her. "You should be resting." He tried to lead her away, his large hand hovering at the small of her back.

"Miss Marrington," Sir Potterfield said as he stepped out of the room where Bennett had been. "I take it that Lord Somersby took great care with your injury?"

Blush warmed her cheeks as she remembered those alone moments with Bennett as he'd tended her wound. "Yes, he did," she managed to say.

"Excellent," Potterfield said. "Now then, I believe we are in agreement to move forward, are we not, Somersby?"

Bennett gave a curt nod, and said nothing. Bennett did not look at her, but she could feel the anger rolling off him in waves.

"What is this next event you would like me to attend?" she asked.

"There is an upcoming art opening that Her Majesty has been supporting. For her to not attend would be suspicious," Potterfield said. "Let us return to the palace and get out of this dank tunnel."

The gentleman whom she had not officially met came to her and offered his arm. "Adrian Winthrop, Marquis of St. Giles, my lady, it is a pleasure to finally make your acquaintance."

She took his arm and they followed Potterfield through the tunnel. Ellis hung back with Bennett and they took up the rear.

"I can prepare you for the art exhibit. I do believe Bennett has given up on you, my dear." St. Giles winked at her with a devilish grin.

Together they followed the tunnel that led back to the Privy Council room, where they took seats. Had Bennett given up on her? She didn't want to work with anyone else; she'd come to trust him. The adventure aspect had increasingly become more dangerous, so she'd be a fool to not want to continue working with the largest and strongest man in the group.

Bennett rolled his eyes heavenward. "No, I am only concerned for her wellbeing, something that no one else seems to be considering. The opera is one thing, a contained building, a contained box seat where no one could get to her. This other will be more difficult. Look at what happened on the train platform."

"We can protect her as we would the queen," St. Giles said. "It is our duty. No one will question our being there."

"That is not the point. She is a civilian."

"A civilian who agreed to do this," Evelyn said. "My Lords, I am perfectly capable and happy to continue with this assignment. I trust that you shall keep me protected." Though she did not call him out, she settled her gaze at Bennett, hoping he would reassure her.

Instead it was St. Giles who grinned and put his hand on her arm. "Precisely, she knows what she's about, is prepared for the potential danger."

"And we will most assuredly compensate you, financially, for the additional time," Potterfield said.

She nodded. "But you aren't anticipating any danger, are you? It's an art exhibit, not the sort of place for ruffians."

"Of course not," St. Giles said. He stood. "Then it is settled. She agrees to continue working and I can get her prepared. I shall see you tomorrow to give you all the instruction you need."

Bennett's jaw clinched. "I never said I was walking away from this assignment. Miss Marrington is my responsibility." He stood and held his hand out to her. "Now, if you will excuse us, I am going to take her back to her chambers so she can rest."

• • •

She turned on him as soon as they were alone in her chamber. "Why don't you want me working with him? He seems as capable as you. Is he not?" Her hands fisted on her hips.

"His capability is not the issue." He did his best to keep his tone even. "You may not work with him. That is the end of the discussion."

"I don't understand. You don't want to continue working with me, yet you refuse to allow someone else to ready me for the event."

"Adrian is a rogue. You will fall in love with him and then he'll break your heart. Is that what you want?"

She covered her mouth with her hand, but mirth glowed in her eyes, and then she laughed, loud and full, a laugh that came from the bottom of her toes.

He frowned. "What is so funny? You believe yourself incapable of falling in love? I can assure you that St. Giles has left a string of broken hearts throughout London and the nearby villages."

"You told me the other day that you do not even believe in love. 'It is merely an illusion of manipulation,' I believe you said. You are a silly man."

"I am not silly. I am trying to protect you." He tossed his arms up in the air. "Evidently, I'm the only one around here who is the least bit concerned about your safety. You are not accustomed to life in London or the ways of the men here."

"He is so different from you?"

"I will not try to seduce you." Not because he didn't want to. Damnation, he wanted to right here, right now. "I will not make you fall in love with me and then break your heart."

"You are such a gentleman." She stepped over to him and reached out to touch his arm, then pulled back. "I shall not fall in love with Lord St. Giles. You have my word." Then she shook her head and smiled. "Besides, I can nearly guarantee that he would not try to seduce me. I've managed to live this long with nary an attempted seduction. I doubt that my presence in London will change that. I am not that tempting." And as if to prove herself, she leaned up on her toes and pressed her lips to his. The kiss was short and chaste, and then she stepped back with a smug little grin on her face.

"See? Even when I behave scandalously, I can't tempt a man."

But that one little taste proved too tempting for him to ignore. He grabbed her and pressed himself against her. "You have no idea how tempting you are." He dropped his mouth to hers. Her lips felt as though they'd been made for him to kiss, an intoxicating combination of satin soft skin and innocence and sweet Evelyn.

Only Evelyn.

She tasted sweet, and the moment her mouth opened to his, the instant her tongue tentatively slid against his, desire forged through him. But it was more than lust; it was an overwhelming sense of protectiveness, possessiveness.

He backed her up, one slow step at a time until he felt her legs bump against the side of her bed. From here, there was nowhere to go but down. Everything about her was intoxicating—the taste of her skin on his lips, the scent of her that was somehow simultaneously exotic and familiar, the innocent, yet seductive way she bumped against him, as if she couldn't get enough of the feel of his body against hers. As if she wanted him to take her right here, in this very moment.

He couldn't take her, though, despite the fact that he knew she'd freely give him whatever he sought. She was his for the taking. It was a heady thought, one that nearly buckled him to his knees. Somehow he found the strength needed to end the kiss. He pressed his forehead to hers. Their labored breaths mingled between them and he gripped her arms.

"I shall not apologize for that because I wouldn't mean it. I wanted to kiss you," he said.

She said nothing, but her head bobbed against his in a nod.

"I want even more, but it is not mine for the taking."

She opened her mouth to say something, but he cupped her face, pulled back from her to look into her eyes. "Please don't offer me anything. I am not so much a gentleman that I won't take it, and there is no honor left in me to do what is right on the other side of the morrow. Suffice it to say, I shall endeavor to not take liberties with you in the future. Perhaps you can be strong enough for both of us and shove me off you next time I come too near."

"Bennett," she whispered.

Beg me to stay.

He kissed her forehead and then forced himself to walk away from her. Seducing Evie would be the worst thing he could do now. His attraction to her was already clouding his ability to do his job appropriately. Potterfield had been right about everything. Getting too close to Evie would prevent him from being able to protect her, and he couldn't bear it if she was injured again.

"Get some sleep," he whispered, then he slipped out of her room.

Chapter Nine

I want even more, but it is not mine for the taking.

She sat on the edge of the bed, put her fingers to her lips. They still hummed with his kiss. Evelyn's mind spun and her heart drummed erratically.

He'd wanted more of her, begged her not to offer herself to him, as if he'd known she had been about to do precisely that. What did she need with her virtue? She had no sentimental reasons to harbor it, save it for some hoped-for love that would rush in and rescue her from her dull life. Besides, hadn't Bennett done that? Pulled her out of the boredom, the incessant nagging from her well-intentioned mother, saved her from the never-ending discussions on hair ribbons and fabric?

Heat spread through her scalp and down her neck as she remembered the scandalous things she had done with her tongue. She had no idea kissing could be like that. Passionate and…good heavens she'd nearly wrapped her legs around him and climbed him as she'd climbed trees when she'd been but a girl.

She tossed herself back on her bed. It seemed quite clear that Bennett and Potterfield had had some sort of confrontation, and somehow in the midst of that St. Giles offered to take over working with her. Bennett had been jealous, hadn't he? Hadn't that been why he'd protested so much about her working with St. Giles? It seemed silly to her that he'd spent a moment worrying about her falling in love with Adrian when it didn't occur to him to protect her heart from himself. Wasn't he the true danger to her heart?

She had no desire to spend any time with St. Giles or anyone else. She'd thought of little besides Bennett since she'd first seen him and his impossibly broad shoulders and dark scowling face. She'd actually come to find that scowl of his endearing.

Still, she needed to gather her wits about her. If she was to become a successful authoress, she did not have time in her life for a man. And he'd certainly made it abundantly clear that he had no need, nor desire for a wife.

Be strong for us both, he'd said.

She'd have to do precisely that. If she wanted to be a writer, she'd have to ignore what her body wanted, and focus on her mind. That shouldn't be too difficult. Certainly that's what she'd been doing all these years, it was only that Bennett had awakened some sort of hunger inside her and she needed only to quiet it again.

Right now her focus was on the next assignment as Her Majesty. Then eventually she could take the money they'd pay her and buy herself a little cottage somewhere, settle in, and write until her heart's content.

She'd spent so much time the night before reliving Bennett's kiss that it had taken until this morning for the anger to surge. While she waited for him to appear, she'd formulated what she'd say to him. So the moment he stepped into the parlor that adjoined the Queen's bedchamber, she stood and spoke.

"I believe you owe me some answers," she said before she could run out of courage to do so. She had only been angry a handful of times in her life. Today was one of those times. "I'm not certain why I didn't bother asking them last night."

He stopped walking and looked at her.

"Exactly why am I here? Where is the Queen and why is someone trying to hurt her?" Then she put her hands over her mouth. "Oh dear, has she already been killed?" Why had it even taken her so long to ask these questions?

He shut the door behind him, then shook his head. "No, of course not, she is relatively unharmed."

"Bennett, please, I was told this was to be a simple assignment and I've been here longer, and—"

"Yes, I know." His jaw clinched, the muscles ticked against his cheeks. He was so dashing, it was distracting. "Victoria is healing from a simple fall. She is safe."

"Yet, I am not."

He released a long breath. "It is the price we pay."

"Not me, I didn't exactly agree to any of this." She hadn't realized how much the events of the railway ceremony had affected her until the words left her mouth. The wound at her side stabbed pain through her when she moved her arms. She was frightened, no sense in denying that. She'd been attacked yesterday, nearly killed, or at the very least she could have been killed. "I thought this was a charade, a taste of adventure from my regular life, a little acting for some money."

"Yes, I realize." He took a step towards her. "Evelyn," he said, his voice softening. "None of this was supposed to happen."

"Look at me, look at all of these things." She picked up a book from one of the occasional tables. "None of this is mine. I'm not even wearing my own undergarments," she said, her voice cracking with emotion.

"But as we discovered earlier, that was helpful in preventing you from being injured worse than you were," he said.

She shook her head. "That is neither here nor there. The fact is, I'm feeling a little overwhelmed by all of this." She gave him a weak smile. "I'm not certain why it took so long for me to fully grasp all of this." She sucked in a breath, but it didn't seem to fill her lungs. "I can't breathe."

He took her over to the settee and lowered her down. "Breathe, Evie, all will be well. I will keep you safe, I promise. But if you want to return, I shall bring you home."

"What of the assignment? I know you fought with Potterfield."

His brows rose, then he shrugged. "I can handle matters with Potterfield. That being said, I've told the other members of the Brotherhood I believe you need to be returned home, but now that you're injured we would have to explain to your family how you happened to get cut in such an interesting place."

She waved her hand dismissively. "That is easily enough explained." Was she ready to return home? She might be frightened, but not so much that she was too scared to stay.

"If Her Majesty isn't healed, then I need to stay until she can return. Do you know when that will be?"

"I do not."

"Do you know who is trying to hurt her?"

He shook his head. "I don't know that either, but it is abundantly clear that someone is definitely trying to harm her. Kill her." He leveled his gaze on her, the weight of his brown eyes was intense, but she did not dare look away. "I am not supposed to discuss such matters with you."

"Me, specifically, or those who do not work for the Crown? Because, it would seem that for however long I do, in fact, work for the Crown. Temporarily."

A ghost of a smile crossed his lips. "I suppose you're correct. Excellent argument, by the by." He was quiet for several moments before he moved to one of the chairs and sat. He motioned for her to do the same. "A few weeks ago, Victoria attended the Royal Ascot where she tripped and fell, injuring herself. Only her ankle, but it prevented her from walking perfectly. And the public already doubts her abilities."

"So you thought to hide her whilst she healed."

He leaned forward, braced his elbows on his knees. "Something like that. Originally we thought to cancel her upcoming events, but then Ellis suggested you."

"Ever since he first met her, he has said I looked exactly like her."

"You favor her," he said with a tight nod, "but there are differences."

The queen, no doubt, was much prettier with softer features. Bennett had commented on her own wild hair on more than one occasion. Evie stood and walked to one of the windows. She missed being able to go outside whenever she chose. Bennett came to stand behind her; she could see his reflection in the window. "Why did you kiss me yesterday?" She turned to face him. "Is it because I remind you of her?"

A deep line furrowed his brow. "What?"

She shrugged. "I thought that might be why."

"No, I could never kiss the Queen. That would be most improper."

He seemed almost insulted she would suggest such a thing, but a stand-in such as herself didn't present a dilemma. That was the only explanation she could think of. "You are a conundrum."

"That is doubtful." He took a step closer to her. "A man does not require a reason to kiss a woman."

"Well, that is ridiculous. One does not simply go around kissing people because the opportunity presents itself. There must be attraction or desire, or at the very least curiosity."

He stepped closer, fingered one of the ringlets that had escaped her hairpins. "You have this all figured out."

"I pay attention to people. They rarely act without first being motivated by something."

"So those are my three options: attraction, desire, or curiosity?"

She shrugged. "Three possible options."

"Well, why did you kiss me?"

"Because you kissed me first."

"So you were being polite?" Again he toyed with the curl by her ear.

She wanted him to kiss her again, but she'd not dare ask for such a thing.

"I meant the first kiss. You leaned up and kissed me, briefly, but a kiss nonetheless. That is the one I was referring to," he said.

"I…that is…you are irritating."

He chuckled.

Surprise and something warm and pleasant curled through her belly. "That's the first time I've seen you laugh. I didn't think you ever did."

"Everyone laughs on occasion. I reserve it for the moments I find truly humorous."

"And my finding you irritating does it?"

He shrugged and that combined with his grin gave him a boyish look about him. "Evidently."

"I'm back to my original assessment of you. A conundrum."

"Very well, I shall remain a conundrum." He dropped the curl and stepped away from her. "Now, we have some additional training to ready you."

She frowned. "For the art exhibit?"

"Not precisely. More of a preventative training measure." He went and stood in the open area of the room. He shifted two chairs out of the way, creating a larger space free of furnishings. "Come here."

She eyed him warily, but walked over to him.

"I want you to hit me."

"Pardon me?"

"Hit me, Evie, as hard as you can, wherever you think is appropriate." Then he held up a hand. He removed his jacket and waistcoat. "Now, whenever you are ready."

"You want me to strike you?"

"Yes."

"Bennett, what is this about?"

"I want you prepared to defend yourself if necessary."

Fear and something akin to excitement coiled through

her. She'd never struck anyone before, not even one of her sisters, but she had certainly read some books with the occasional tussle. She took in the sight of the man before her. He stood, unguarded, with his arms at his sides. Slapping him would be the easiest, but she doubted that's what he meant by defending herself.

"How do I hold my hand?"

He grinned. "However you wish."

She closed her fingers into a fist and with as much strength as she could muster, and she punched him right in the stomach. The rock hard wall of his abdomen didn't budge beneath her strike. "Good heavens, you are no different than a wall."

"You went straight for the most obvious place. The trick is to size up your opponent and try to determine his more vulnerable areas."

She allowed her gaze to travel the long length of him. He was massive: tall, broad, and hard. "I seem unable to find any vulnerable areas."

His lips quirked in a grin. "Consider the eyes. You can jab a man in the eyes. That will give him pause. Ladies also possess the unique skill of being able to scratch an opponent. So look for such things." He positioned himself closer to her. "Now then, what do you do if someone grabs you?" He did, pulling her to him and holding her close to his body.

She was supposed to fight, that's what this exercise was for. But here, pressed firmly against his muscular frame, she felt no hurry to escape. She resisted the urge to sigh and rest her head against him. She wiggled to try and free herself, but his grip became manacles and she could not budge. *Look for vulnerabilities.* Well, she couldn't see his face from their current position so she did the only thing she could think of—she jumped and stomped on his boots. The movement jarred her free and she turned to face him. "Aha!" she said.

His eyes had grown darker and the muscles in his jaw ticked an erratic rhythm. "You can also kick, bite, whatever you can to break free. You might want to not wiggle so much if a man has you pressed against him."

She nodded. "Do you train the monarchs in self protection?"

• • •

He took the opportunity to move away from her. There was only so much temptation a man could endure. Her voluptuous curves pressed against him like that and he'd completely forgotten the point of the exercise. He'd wanted nothing more to do than dip his head down and taste her bare neck, nibble at the curve of her shoulder. He'd released her as soon as he'd been able. Maybe he should have had Adrian train her in this. Perhaps he could restrain himself.

He stood near the sitting area, hoping she would sit. As it was, he had to hope she did not notice his erection straining against his trousers. Damnation, but he wanted her.

"Bennett?" she asked.

She had asked him a question, something about training the monarchs. "In the past the Brotherhood have traditionally given some basic training to the kings, enough that they are able to protect themselves."

"And Her Majesty?" Evie asked.

"She is the first Queen in over a century, the first Queen since the inception of the Brotherhood." He shook his head. "No, we have given her no training. She was bred a genteel lady."

"True, but someone is trying to kill her." Evie walked over to him, placed her hand on his forearm. "You need to give her a fighting chance."

The touch was more than he could bear. He pulled her to him and she stilled, looked up at his face.

"Am I to find a way out of your hold while facing you?" she asked.

"I had something else in mind." He lowered his lips to hers.

She was pliant and soft beneath him, had even leaned in closer to him. He teased at her bottom lip with his teeth and then his tongue until she parted and allowed him entrance.

He kept things slow and gentle, seductively worshiping her mouth. She sighed into his mouth, and a deep satisfaction surged through his body and he tightened his grasp on her. Desire, thick and hot took over his body.

She met his intensity, kissed him back with equal parts urgency and innocence. He wanted to caress her, slip his hand beneath her bodice, find her skin, soft and pliant, but he held his desire in check. He shouldn't be kissing her, but he'd needed one more taste. He wouldn't go too far, not with this one. She was different. She needed his protection, and it was becoming clearer that she needed protection from him.

Her fingers dug into his shoulders and she gripped him.

A light rap came to the door and Bennett released her.

"Somersby," Adrian said from the other side. "Potterfield wants to see you."

"I'll be there in a minute," Bennett called. "All you need remember is to fight as best you can to get away from someone if they attack you." Then he tilted his head and swore. "And perhaps you should start defending yourself against an earl who seems to have trouble keeping his hands off you."

Chapter Ten

Evelyn woke from a deep sleep with chills biting at her flesh. Her eyes opened, but the room was too dark to see much past her hand. She lay still, listening. A floorboard creaked and she had barely registered that someone was in the room with her before they were upon her, pinning her down.

Bile rose in her throat and panic surged through her limbs. She swung her arms, aimlessly throwing herself against her assailant in an effort to get him off her. She screamed as loudly as she could. "Help! Help me!"

He slammed his hand down on her mouth and she bit into his hand, not caring about the filth, only wanting to do something, anything to save herself. The metallic taste of his blood filled her mouth and she spat it at him.

"You bitch!"

He hit her head with something heavy and pain shot through her skull, piercing the back of her eyes. She tried to scream again, but he muffled her mouth with some piece of clothing. Still she fought. And then as quickly as he'd appeared, the weight of him lifted. There was a huge crash to her right. She sat up, gasping for breath. "Who's there?" She didn't know if she should stand, get out of bed, or stay where she sat. Fear settled heavy on her and she pulled the coverlet to her, wrapping her arms around her bent legs.

Other footsteps entered the room. "Someone light a bloody lamp." It was Bennett.

Her nerves splintered and tears pricked her eyes as relief washed over her.

Light illuminated across the room and she peered around the curtains of the bed. Bennett held some man on the ground, his right foot pressed into the man's throat. Two other members of the Brotherhood entered.

"Who sent you?" Bennett asked, pressing his boot hard into the man's throat.

The man made a choking sound.

"He won't be able to answer any questions as long as you're stepping on this neck," Adrian said. He walked over to Bennett. He reached down and grabbed the man up by the shirtfront and lifted him to his feet. "You tend to her and we'll take this one down to answer some questions."

Bennett watched as the other men carried her assailant out of the room. He appeared so unassuming. Had she seen the man on the street, she would have figured him married with a few children and that perhaps he worked at a local shop.

Bennett waited until they were alone before facing Evie.

"Are you all right?"

"Am I all right?" Her voice hitched as she spoke. She paced the length of the room, a feat in and of itself because of the large size of the bedchamber. "I accepted this, agreed to this. I wanted the adventure. The experience." She stopped walking and stared and him, then she shook her head and began her journey across the room once more.

He allowed her to pace and talk for another fifteen minutes, though none of her sentences connected or made much sense. As her words fell together faster and her breathing became shorter, he made his way to her, gripped her arms to steady her.

"Evelyn, all is well, you are safe now. I shall not allow anything else to happen to you." He was ready to leave tonight, ready to take her to his townhome and lock her away if need be. Damnation, but she had already been through far too much.

She stared at him, gape mouthed. "But how do you? Where did he come from? I was asleep and then he was here, in my room and then on top of me." She shook her head. "Are there not guards all over this palace?"

"Indeed there are. We're fairly certain how he got in and now guards will be protecting those areas." He led her over to the bed and sat her down. "You need to get some sleep. We can talk more about this in the morning."

She allowed him to lay her back into the bed and pull the coverlet up over her, yet her eyes were wide with fear.

He turned to go.

"Where are you going?" She sat upright.

"I'll be on the other side of those doors."

"Please don't." She shook her head. "I don't want to be alone. Not tonight."

He should leave, he knew that. Staying would be

tempting. As it was he was fighting with his urge to pull her into his arms and hold her until that fear disappeared from her eyes. Leaving was the proper thing to do, but what man could walk away from such a request? She'd just been attacked for the second time in as many days. "I'll stay. You sleep." He walked to the sitting area across the large room and sat.

"You're really quite terrible at providing comfort," she said.

"I beg your pardon?"

"I'm frightened, Bennett, more than that, terrified. I care not for what is proper at the moment. Please come over here and sit on the bed." She sat, looked at him, her large whiskey-colored eyes pleaded with him. "I need you close."

He swallowed. He was already struggling staying in here with her when he wanted to be down below beating the hell out of that man who'd attacked her, finding out who had sent him and what this was all about.

If anyone still had questions after the incident at the train ceremony, they certainly had undeniable proof now that someone was trying to kill the queen, yet all he could think about what Evelyn's safety. He sat on the edge of the bed, as far away from her as possible. He knew if he got any closer he'd pull her to him, search every inch of skin to ensure she was not hurt.

"Did he hurt you?" he asked.

"He hit my head, it throbs still, but there is no wound." She rubbed at her scalp, winced at her own touch.

Her hair fell into a long plait over her left shoulder. Her dressing gown covered nearly every swath of her pale skin. She was beautiful, so much so that his mouth had gone dry.

What kind of man had lustful thoughts after a woman had been through such an ordeal? He was the worst sort of louse.

"I am sorry about this. We never should have brought you here, put you in this kind of danger. I should have fought against their decision to put you into this."

"Were you given such an opportunity? You said once you hadn't had a choice in the matter."

"Not exactly. And I have a history of not following orders, so in this particular situation, I especially had no choice. But that's my burden. It should not have been yours."

She released a half-hearted chuckle. "You know when you told me that the Queen had been in danger before, I didn't truly believe you. I suppose I thought you meant something more stately, as in other countries who were displeased with certain situations. I never considered—" Her chest rose and fell and deep breaths. "And you have been in such danger?"

"Not precisely the same, but I've had my share of situations." He leaned forward a little.

"I can't imagine anyone going after you. They'd have to be a fool." She reached out and grabbed one of his hands. "Tell me about them."

"I don't think that will help in calming you down. Perhaps we could discuss something else."

She nodded, laid her head back down on the pillow. She patted the pillow next to her. "Come up here so I can see you."

He shifted himself so that he lay across from her, his head resting on a pillow, but his body lay upon the covers rather than beneath with her. He had only so much control. "Earlier when you were talking, you mentioned something about adventure and writing. What were you talking about?"

"Oh, nothing, 'tis foolish."

"Still, tell me, nonetheless. You said that talking would calm you down."

"Very well, though you mustn't laugh." Then she released a slight chuckle. "I don't suppose that is too difficult for you considering you don't find humor in much."

"Precisely. I am rather stoic." She smiled and it was so genuine it made his chest hurt.

"I want to be a writer. No, I am a writer. Adventure stories." She rolled her eyes heavenward. "And I foolishly thought this would be good experience to assist with my stories. I thought that pretending to be someone else for a while, living a different life would give me perspective, ideas, inspiration, if you will."

"I suppose that makes sense. It is likely easier to write about something if you've experienced it. And has this given you any inspiration or have you decided that the adventurous life isn't for you?"

"Yes, I've had an idea or two." Sadness fell over her eyes. "I don't believe I can give up the writing, though I don't suppose I'm equipped to do anything else."

She made no mention of wanting to find a husband, have children and house to keep.

"I wanted to experience anything other than my mundane country life."

"I'd wager that life is looking pretty good about now," he said, unable to hide his own grin.

"Indeed. And the money from this will help."

Ah yes, the money. "In what way?"

"Enable me to find a little cottage somewhere, live on my own, and not have to marry. It is the only way my father will allow me to forego marriage with some unpleasant old man. I must be financially sound else he will force me to find a husband."

He couldn't imagine Evie living alone somewhere in a cottage. Either her father was a fool, or he'd never counted on her finding such financial solvency. "A woman needs to be cared for."

"Perhaps, but they don't have to have a man to accomplish such things."

There was a possibility, as slight as it might be, that he was wrong about Evelyn. Perhaps she wasn't like all other women and only after a man's money. Yes, she needed funds, but for practical reasons. He certainly couldn't fault her there.

"Would you do something for me, if I asked?" she asked.

"I would try."

"Would you hold me for a little while? I can't shake the sensations of that man touching me."

She was a wicked temptress, asking him such a thing, but the weariness and fear in her face called to him. He did as she requested, much to his concern. His control was wearing thin, now with her body pressed against his, he wasn't sure he could withstand the temptation.

"Thank you for coming to my rescue. Again," she said.

And that turned out to be his undoing. He lowered his mouth to hers and kissed her, gently at first, to make her feel safe and secure. But when her lips parted and he felt the tip of her tongue slide seductively across his bottom lip, it was all he could stand.

He pulled her to him so that she was half lying, half leaning across him. He moved his mouth down on hers, simultaneously seducing and worshipping. He'd hoped he'd be able to be in here with her without having to touch her, but he'd never been very good at resisting temptation.

He needed her near, needed to touch her, kiss her, as a parched man needed drink. He slid his tongue through her teeth, sweeping it across her own. His hand held her head in place, and his other caressed her bare shoulder where her dressing gown had slipped aside. She was so seductive, yet she knew not how tempting she could be. It made the experience all the more exciting, knowing that no one yet had noticed her beguiling ways. It was as if he'd unlocked her secret.

He continued kissing her, loving the feel of her soft body pressed against his, the way her mouth yielded to him. She kissed him back, giving as much as he gave, and the sensations were heady, addictive. If he could kiss her like this every day, he'd be tempted to go back on his pledge to remain unmarried and take her straight to the church. Sensations such as these were why people married in haste.

Her hands slid up around his neck, pulling him down further upon her. He was only half atop her, the other half of him on his side of the bed, and still the bed covers lay between them. It gave her some measure of protection from his obvious lack of control.

He longed to slide his hands up her legs to the center of her—to explore and see if she was wet for him, as wet as he was hard. His mouth left hers and he trailed kisses down her jaw to the column of her throat and then down her neck, across her collarbone to her shoulder, where he nipped lightly.

She released soft, sweet sounds of pleasure, then sighed

contentedly as he continued his perusal of her body. She kicked at the covers pinning her to the bed, but he offered her no assistance. Instead, he kissed the tops of her breasts, where her labored breathing had them rising and falling. Her flesh was so perfectly plump, he couldn't stand it any longer. With a quick maneuver he pushed aside the dressing gown, freeing her breasts. She sucked in a breath, but said nothing in protest.

They were perfect, round and full, and perfectly pink tipped. He dipped his head and took one nipple in his mouth. The hard, erect little nub beaded against his tongue. Her hands gripped at his shoulders and she arched up toward him, pressing her breast farther into his mouth. Again she kicked at the covers.

He wanted nothing more than to lose himself in her, but he knew that couldn't happen. She was a virgin, and despite his temptations otherwise, he would not offer her marriage. Therefore he would not take what was offered to him. Still he wanted her, and she obviously wanted him, so he'd give her a little more, then he'd force himself to walk away.

He moved himself so that he was fully atop her, pressed his erection against the apex of her thighs. Even with the covers between them, she could feel him.

Christ, she felt good. It would take nothing to whip the covers out from between them, unfasten his trousers, and bury himself inside her. She'd be warm and wet and tight, and he nearly lost himself with that single thought.

He kissed at her throat, cupped her breast, then kissed her again, all the while moving against her. He could imagine her wetness against him, though he knew it was nothing but his imagination. There were far too many layers between them. Still, the hard ridge of him rubbed her in the right spot. Her knees opened wider, giving him more room, and she whimpered and squirmed while her nails bit into shoulders.

He knew in that moment that walking away from her would be the hardest thing he'd ever do, but he also knew that no matter what, he'd have to take his leave. He had no promises for a woman like Evie.

Her climax hit and she tossed her head back and gasped again and again while the pleasure rocketed through her. When her pleasure subsided, she opened her eyes and looked at him as if he were some sort of hero. He rolled off her and snuggled in behind her, wrapping his arms tightly around her. She needed sleep and he needed to not look into her eyes.

• • •

Bennett was thankful once she had fallen asleep. He had put distance between himself and Evelyn. Currently, he sat in a chair across the wide expanse of the Queen's bedchamber. There was a slight rap at the door, and then it cracked open. Adrian slipped inside.

"We have a problem," he said.

"What?" Bennett came to his feet.

"The man has escaped."

Bennett swore louder than he intended and Evelyn sat upright in the bed, clutching the bedding to her bare chest. Thankfully the curtains that canopied the bed mostly hid her.

"Bennett?" she asked, her voice etched in fear.

"I'm here." He walked over to her. "You need to get up

and come with me."

"Where are we going?"

He handed her the dressing gown and she slipped it on.

"Back down below, somewhere you should never have known about." He and Adrian led her over to the large bookshelf that lined one entire wall of the bedchamber. He shifted a book on the third shelf from the top and it clicked, then the bookshelf slid open and revealed a staircase leading downward. "When they were building this palace, with the intent to be the London residence for the royal family, we had a series of tunnels built beneath so we could always be at hand whenever we were needed."

He led her down. "So there are others in addition to the one off of the Privy Council room?"

"There's a veritable maze of them," Bennett said.

"Ellis went after the man," Adrian said quietly so that only Bennett could hear. "But I doubt he'll find him. The bastard knew these tunnels as if he had built them himself."

They moved quickly through the tunnels, the chill permeating his skin and he knew Evie was likely freezing. He took off his jacket and wrapped it around her shoulders. "Could he have been one of the workers?" Bennett asked.

"Honestly, I don't know. We were so careful with the hiring of those workers. It seems unlikely."

They continued walking through the tight stone tunnels. "How are you doing, Evelyn?" Bennett asked.

"I shall survive. We are going in further than we did the last time," she said.

"Yes, that area is below the Privy Council room. These are the main tunnels, the ones that lead in and out of the royal family's sleeping quarters."

"I can say that I don't particularly care for small, confined spaces though."

"Nor I."

"At least I can walk upright. It's a wonder you haven't hit your head," she said.

"Today I haven't, but that doesn't mean it hasn't happened before."

"On more than one occasion," Adrian said with mirth in his voice.

Bennett caught Evelyn's grin before it faded and was replaced with a furrowed look of concentration.

They finally came to the series of doors that housed some of the offices of the Brotherhood.

"You can sit anywhere." Adrian pointed to several chairs that encircled a large table. "Allow me to officially welcome you to *Custos a Vesica*."

"Brotherhood of the blade?" she asked.

"Ah, you know your Latin fairly well. Brotherhood of the Sword, actually." Bennett rolled his eyes. "It was a name given to us many years ago." He looked around the room. "Where the hell is everyone?"

"Perhaps they went with Ellis to search for the man."

"He escaped?" Evelyn asked, her eyes wide with fright.

"Indeed, but we shall find him," Adrian said.

"She needs to be moved somewhere else secure. I'm taking her to my townhome," Bennett said. "But first I want some answers. Was the man not restrained?"

Adrian sighed. "He was, but evidently when we searched him, we missed some sort of blade that he used to cut himself free."

"Morton," Bennett said. "We need him here. Now."

"You think he's part of this?" Adrian asked.

"There's a very good chance he knows something." Bennett quickly filled him in on Gwyneth's attempt at blackmail and then Morton's subsequent visit to Evie.

Adrian nodded. "I'll go find him myself then." He bowed to Evelyn and then left them alone.

"We'll wait for Potterfield and then I'm moving you to my townhome." Bennett was thankful a table separated him from Evelyn since he hadn't been able to control himself earlier, and all he wanted to do was pull her back into his arms and hold her until her eyes were no longer filled with fear.

· · ·

"What do we do now?" Evelyn asked him. Too much had happened tonight. Her body felt pulled and scraped in so many directions. First the attack, and then the tender and passionate moments with Bennett, and now her attacker had escaped. No, not hers, but rather, the Queen's. Perhaps it truly was time for Evelyn to go home.

There was a ruckus down the tunnel that sounded like it came from the stairs. Instantly Bennett was between her and the doorway, a pistol in his hand.

"Honestly, Percival, there is no need to fuss. I am capable of descending steps," a woman's voice echoed down to them.

"Victoria," Bennett whispered.

"The Queen? She is here? Now?" Evelyn wrapped the dressing gown tighter about her, then pulled Bennett's coat closed. She patted the long fiery braid that fell over her shoulder. She was going to meet the Queen, the woman she had been impersonating. Nerves surged up her throat threatening to choke her. "My mother would have a fit of the vapors if she knew I was going to meet our monarch looking like this."

"Relax," Bennett said. "It is not yet dawn, so what else would you look like?"

"Relax," she repeated dumbly. "I do not think that is poss—"

"There you are, Bennett. Percival here has been filling me in on the details of all that has transpired over the last week or so," the Queen said. Then her eyes landed on Evelyn. "Oh, is this her?" She didn't wait for an answer, merely stepped forward and grabbed Evelyn's hands. "My goodness you do favor me, except you quite obviously have much better hair than I do. I'm afraid mine is so thin and fine, I can scarcely do anything with it."

Evelyn bent in a deep curtsey. "Your Majesty."

"While I appreciate your show of ceremony, I do believe we're beyond that. You have been wearing my clothes and sleeping in my bed, have you not?"

Evelyn felt her cheeks grow warm. "Yes."

"See then." Victoria linked her arm with Evelyn's. "We are practically the best of friends, I should say."

Evelyn relaxed and smiled. Victoria was young and pretty, and Evelyn could see similarities to their features.

"I trust that my cousin has been taking good care of you?" Victoria eyed Bennett suspiciously, then gave him a wink.

"Yes, quite good. He has saved me on more than one occasion."

"So I have heard." The Queen frowned at the two men who stood quiet and still. "I am so very grateful for your service, my dear. You will be compensated handsomely for your sacrifice."

Evelyn didn't know what to say so she merely nodded.

"I shall be taking over now that my ankle is healed. Quite honestly, I believe these men made much out of nothing."

"Your reputation—"

"Is what?" Victoria asked, her brows raised in a perfect arch. "It matters not what they think or what they say. I am Queen. What more can they do about it now?" She gave Evelyn a wink and an impish grin, reminding her precisely how young the Queen was.

"We can clear your schedule and tell everyone you have gone on holiday," Potterfield said.

"We will do no such thing. I am not going to hide out simply because some lunatic tried to kill me." She squeezed Evelyn's arm. "Well, you dear, and you must be horribly frightened."

"I was, but I am much better now." Evelyn's eyes met Bennett's across the room and she would have sworn that heat radiated off his body and slid over to her own.

Victoria faced Bennett. "You shall deliver our dear Miss Marrington safely back to her family with my thanks."

Bennett nodded. "The assailant is still out there, Your Majesty."

"I have complete faith that your men will find him and imprison him," Victoria said.

And that was it. Evelyn had been dismissed. Certainly appreciated for her service, but in an instant her adventure had come to an end. She couldn't say she was that disappointed considering she'd been attacked twice. She'd lived an adventure and had experienced true fear enough to write about it with authenticity.

Chapter Eleven

Bennett intended to bring Evie straight to his townhome in London, but she protested. The Queen had dismissed her and it was time for her to return home.

They spent the better part of the ride to her family's cottage in silence, her reading and periodically looking at the window and him running through scenarios in his mind as to what was happening with the assassin. Well, he had thought about that, but he'd mostly fought with himself and his desire to pull Evelyn into his lap and kiss her the entire way to her cottage. But that was ridiculous, especially now that the charade was over. She was to return to her country life and he would return to London and hope that Potterfield deemed his assignment a success.

"I didn't think you'd ride with me?"

"Pardon?" he asked, rattled by her sudden statement.

"Well, when you brought me from my house, you rode your horse. In the rain. I thought you must have really not wanted to spend time alone with me."

"I—"

"You don't have to say anything." Her delicate shoulders rose in a shrug. "It was merely an observation."

"Are you ready to be home? Have your life back to what you are more accustomed to?" he asked, unsure of what to say.

She sighed. "In many ways, I am ready to be home, but in others, no. I was rather enjoying life in London. I've never been around so many people at once. It was fascinating. People are fascinating. You don't see many different sorts in the country. It's much of the same."

"What will you do now?"

"I'm not certain. I'm hoping that the money will convince my father that I am prepared to care for myself and he won't require me to marry anyone. But my mother can be quite persuasive, so I don't know how that will go. She has her hopes set on my marrying the Viscount Edgerly."

"You do not want to?"

Her lip sneered and she shook her head. "No, of course not. First of all, he's old, practically the same age as my father. Secondly, he's old, though I'm certain there are other reasons." She laughed. "He only wants me to take care of his eleven children."

"Eleven children? That's plenty. You'd most assuredly have your hands full with that brood."

"Indeed. I thought having four sisters was a lot. Imagine having six brothers and five sisters." She shook her head again. "No, thank you."

The carriage turned down the rocky road that led to her family's cottage. The stones cracked and crunched beneath the wheels and she peered out the window, looking very much a mixture of wistful woman and eager child.

"I do feel as if I have been gone from my family for too long. They are big and loud and drive me to near madness, but I cannot help but adore them." She smiled, a smile that cut straight into him.

And then the carriage stopped and he was helping her down from the rig. He gave his driver some instructions and then led her to her front door.

She opened it up. "Mama, Papa, I am home," she called. "Jilly, Meghan? Where is everyone?"

The housekeeper rounded the corner at the end of the corridor. "Oh, Miss Evelyn, whatever are you doing home? Did Catherine not find you in time?"

Bennett stood behind Evie holding the small trunk the Queen had gifted her.

Evelyn frowned. "Catherine? No, she did not."

"Yes, your sister came to see you," the housekeeper said, "at your aunt's in London, to give you the message."

"She came to our aunt's?" Evie repeated. "What message?" Color drained from Evie's face.

"That the entire family was going to Bristol for a special party hosted by Miss Jillian's betrothed's family. Truly fancy. They wanted you to meet them there, so Catherine came to get you."

"Oh dear," Evelyn said.

Bennett reached for her elbow to steady her. "All will be well," he said in a hushed voice.

"Let me fetch some tea. You two can rest in the parlor." Then the housekeeper left them standing there.

"They'll know now that I wasn't with my aunt, that I've

been somewhere else entirely, somewhere they don't know how to find me." Her eyes rounded. "What am I to do?"

"I will send them a message to Lord Bellview and let them know that you—"

"That what?" She spun around to face him. "That I've been living at Buckingham Palace charading as the Queen?" she hissed. "Which I am most certain must be some sort of treason."

"Not if Her Majesty approves of it, which she did."

"Still. What are we going to say?" She bit down on her lip. "My mother will certainly have an apoplexy."

"I shall think of something. In the meantime, I am not leaving you here alone."

"You can most definitely not stay here with me. We have no place." She waved her hand. "Poppycock. I am perfectly safe here with Mrs. Kimble."

"We don't know that. I was charged with your safety and I am not leaving you here without your family. I will not argue this point, Evelyn."

She glared at him. "You are an intimidator, do you know that?"

"Be that as it may, I am determined to keep you safe." And perhaps he wasn't quite ready to rid himself of her just yet, but he would never admit to that. "We shall return to my estate until your family returns. It is not too far from here."

. . .

Several hours later, Bennett sat in his bedchamber, unable to sleep. He'd been in his bed for nearly half an hour before he'd finally gotten up and sat. He'd tried to read, but his attention would not hold. His mind was plagued with thoughts of Evelyn and everything that had transpired over the last two weeks.

So much had changed since the last time they were alone in one of his homes. The last time he hadn't known her, hadn't trusted her. He'd certainly found her attractive then, but now he knew how tempting she could be. He wanted her, there was no denying that.

By the time Mrs. Kimble fed them and sent them on their way, Evie was exhausted. She'd fallen asleep in the carriage and he carried her into an adjacent bedchamber when they arrived at his estate. As for what they'd tell her family—he'd already decided he'd sit her father down and give him some of the details, enough that they'd know she'd not been doing anything untoward.

There was a rap of knuckles on his bedchamber door.

"Enter," he said, expecting it to be his valet. Instead, Evie stepped inside his dim-lit room. He stood.

"Evie, is everything all right?"

She nodded, walked directly to him and put a finger to his lips. "I know I'm not her. I know I'm not the one you want, but perhaps you could pretend because this night is my only chance at this. My only chance to feel passion and not become the prudish spinster."

Evelyn Marrington had come to seduce him. Damnation.

"Evelyn, I don't want her. I never have. It's you I want."

She tilted her head so that she met his lips. Her hands ran up the length of his chest and grabbed the front of his coat, pulling him closer. Bennett kissed her back, slanting his mouth over hers.

Deepening the kiss, Evie darted her tongue out and ran

it against his. She was being bold, brazen, and she loved it. Fireworks sparked through her blood, igniting shocks of pleasure throughout her body. A tingle started at the apex of her thighs and hummed down her legs.

His soft lips responded immediately as she leaned her body into his. She kissed him passionately, threading her fingers through the back of his hair. It was surprisingly soft, a sharp contrast to his solid and toned neck. Bennett's tongue swirled through her mouth, and she heard herself moan.

She reached between them and untied the dressing gown, allowing it to fall to the floor. There was no going back now. She was offering herself completely to him. He would either take her or send her away.

Coils of pleasure sprang from her abdomen and wound up around her to tease and tingle her breasts. His hands, as if her body had whispered to him, found her sensitive nipples. They hardened against his touch.

He kissed her again, but this time he let his mouth trail down her neck to right behind her ear, where he placed tiny licks and bites until she thought she would melt into a puddle at his feet, across her collarbone, down to the swell of her breast.

She arched against him, giving him more access. His hand cupped her breast as he continued to lave kisses on her skin. She moaned again. She wanted to wrap her legs around him and have him make love to her right up against the wall, but she knew Bennett would not hear of it.

His lips trailed to her ear, then down her throat. He cupped her breast, and she arched into him.

"You are so beautiful," he whispered against her hair.

And perhaps it was the headiness of her desire talking,

but she believed him, believed that he found her beautiful.

His hand lifted her slightly by squeezing her bottom, then he nuzzled his face into the crook of her neck. The day's growth of beard scraped tantalizingly against her collarbone as he took small heated nips along the tender flesh.

He moved her to the bed, but before he pressed them to the mattress, he placed both hands on the sides of her face, leaned in and kissed her. Not any kiss, but a kiss intended to imprint itself on a human soul, so tender, so full of yearning, she could not help but cry out. The sound was muffled by his mouth's covering. His tongue slid against her bottom lip, and she opened to him, and lost were her protests as she melted against his body. And then he was gone. He stepped away from her and unfastened his trousers. She took in the sight of him, standing there wearing nothing but a wolfish grin.

She so wanted this, wanted him.

He walked to her and laid them to the mattress. She ran her hands over his torso, touching every hard sinewy line on his chest. She couldn't deny her desire for him any longer. She simply wouldn't.

Her body hummed with lust. Everywhere he touched, fire lit under her skin and blazed through her. Her nipples peaked. She was wet for him, so wet and aching for his touch. For him to be inside her, for him to sate whatever it was her body craved.

He stilled her hand, and met her eyes. "Evie, I can't offer you anything more."

His words tugged at her heart, but she ignored it. He couldn't offer, and she would certainly never ask. "I don't need anything else."

He was so handsome, so rugged, so perfect. She wanted

to touch him everywhere.

"You don't know how much I want you," he said, his voice raw with desire. He grabbed her hand and pulled her back to him so that their bodies pressed together, flesh upon flesh. "How I've wanted you from the moment I laid eyes on you in that ballroom."

His hands cupped her bottom, pressing her to him, pressing her into his erection. She kissed him again, then wrapped her legs around his waist, encouraging him to get closer, to lose himself inside her.

It was all the encouragement he needed. With slow and steady movements, he entered her. The fullness of him felt so right, so exactly what she needed, what she craved. In that moment she wished it could be like this forever, the two of them together, hidden away from the world, but she knew tonight was their only night.

His movements were deep and sensual, and her climax began to build almost immediately. Swifter and swifter, she climbed until she couldn't hold it any longer, and the world seemed to shatter in a million glassy fragments all around her. She clung to his shoulders as the pleasures rocked her, and she was vaguely aware of his own climax as his abdomen tightened against her.

• • •

Bennett had not seen Evelyn yet and it was nearing noon. Of course he'd kept her up virtually all night making love to her again and again. And they'd talked, so easily, about her family, his family, his ambitions with the Brotherhood and her writing.

It had been a perfect night. But now as he sat behind his desk in his study, the night seemed almost a fantasy. In the light of the day, though, he was questioning his actions. He'd taken her virtue and had no intentions of doing anything honorable about that. She'd asked him to make love to her, insisted she had no fantasies of marrying, she'd simply wanted him for the night.

"My Lord," his butler said after rapping on the study door. "Your mother is here and requests an audience with you."

"My mother?" He nodded. "Very well, send her in."

Bennett stood and waited. More than likely she had come to tell him of her next marriage. She'd been spending a fair amount of time with Lord Beckwith, he'd heard. Perhaps the earl had asked and his mother would be walking down the marital aisle for the fourth time.

"Bennett, love, you know how I do hate coming to the country. Why do you not stay in London more often?"

"I've been in London for the past several weeks and only arrived here yesterday," he said. He motioned for her to take a seat and asked his butler to have tea sent in.

"Still, I had to go there first and then was told to come here and it's such an uncomfortably long drive." She lowered herself onto the floral wingback chair. She was still a handsome woman, with nary a wrinkled line marring her aging face.

"It takes no more than two and a quarter hours, Mother. It is not as if the estate is in Wales."

"Thank the heavens." She shuddered. "That would be miserable. Out there in that rugged land."

"What do you want?"

She had the decency to look offended. "Can a mother not visit her son with no reason other than to see his handsome face?" She straightened her skirts, pursed her lips.

"Perhaps some mothers, but not mine."

She held firm for the briefest of moments, before her shoulders fell and she smiled. "You do know me so well."

"Indeed." The teacart was brought in and Bennett poured his mother a cup, then handed it over to her. "Now then, out with it, Mother."

"Very well," she said as she stirred the sugar into her tea. "I have heard a most delicious rumor."

"Why you would travel all the way here to tell me is rather baffling. You know I cannot abide gossip, nor should you. We have seen how damaging gossip can be." How quickly she seemed to forget his sister. "I can assure you that I am not the least bit interested."

"I think you should make an exception, considering this rumor is about you." She sipped her tea.

"And you are somehow pleased about this?"

She frowned. "No, I certainly found the tale amusing, but when I realized it was attached to your name, I came to find you straight away to inform you."

Out of the kindness of her heart, no doubt, and not because she wanted to see if whatever it was had merit. "I appreciate your concern for my good name, but I care not what people say about me."

"It is not merely you, there is a certain young woman whose name is being linked to yours and it would seem that you have ruined it."

"Ruined who, precisely? Because I can assure you I have done nothing of the sort." And then memories of the night before and Evie's cries of passion, her lovely fair skin marred with the blush of arousal, flashed through his mind. He bit back a swear.

"A country miss. I am not certain I recall her name." She waved her hands dismissively, "But it would seem that she was supposed to be caring for an ailing aunt and instead has not been seen or heard from since leaving her cottage, nearly three weeks ago. With you. What have you done with her, Bennett?"

How the hell had that traveled all the way to London? "This is a misunderstanding, nothing more."

Her brows rose. "So you know of the girl?"

"What girl?" Evelyn asked from the doorway.

Splendid. She had impeccable timing. Bennett stood. "Mother, may I present Miss Evelyn Marrington."

"Yes, that was her name."

Evelyn came forward, blush creeping up to stain her cheeks. "My Lady, so lovely to meet you." She curtsied and his mother didn't even bother to stand.

"So it is not a rumor at all. Good heavens, Bennett, you may do as you wish and have elicit affairs, but be discreet and perhaps more selective."

"I'm sorry, I could have sworn that you just counseled me to be more discreet with my affairs? Honestly, mother, that is laughable with all of the cavorting you do in London."

She came to her feet then. "I believe I shall retire for a while before returning to London. It is such a tiring drive. And then to have my only child be so very rude."

Evelyn stood there, mouth agape, watching as his mother left the room. He followed her out, leaving Evie alone.

"Mother, first, I am not your only child. You do not get

to pretend that Christy never existed simply because she is dead. Secondly, that was most unkind."

"Your sister was weak, and I do not mention her because it is too painful to do so."

He doubted that, but said no more about the matter.

She waved her hand dismissively. "I was stating the truth. That girl is obviously trying to trap you into a marriage that would only benefit her. There's certainly nothing you would gain from saddling yourself with a country miss."

"You have no notion of what you're talking about."

"Considering I have been that girl, the advantageous girl with no funds and a pretty face. It is quite easy to trap men into a marriage, but you, my dear, can certainly do better. You are so handsome." She patted his cheek.

He withdrew from her touch. "That's not what I meant. My relationship with Miss Marrington is far more evolved. We are to be married." The words were out of his mouth before he'd fully considered them, but he knew, without a doubt, that it was what had to be done. He had ruined her, and it would seem that the world knew about it. He would do the honorable thing and marry her.

"Bennett, do not ruin your life on a girl such as this. Yes, people will believe that you have defiled her. You must take her home immediately. Certainly her family can think of a way to salvage her reputation."

"Listen to yourself, Mother." He wanted to tell her the truth to defend Evelyn; tell his mother about the assignment with the Brotherhood. But that would betray every oath he'd taken for the Brotherhood. He shook his head. "I'll see that your horses are tended and your carriage is ready for you to return to London first thing tomorrow morning." He turned on his heel and stepped back into his study.

Evelyn still stood in the very same spot.

He wanted to be able to say that his mother meant well, that her intentions were well meaning, but the truth was, she'd come here to appease her own curiosity and no other reason.

He was angry as hell about the entire situation. This was what he'd worked so hard to prevent. After Gwyneth, he never wanted to be put in this kind of situation, where a woman was after his name for his money. And here he was embroiled in a scandal of his own making. He had no choice. He would have to do the honorable thing.

• • •

"I didn't mean to interrupt. I hadn't realized your mother arrived," Evelyn said.

"She doesn't normally visit."

"Would it be too much trouble to ready a carriage for me? I believe it is beyond time I return home."

"Nonsense. Once your family has returned, but until then you are quite welcomed here." His words were kind, but the tone in his voice suggested he wanted her anywhere but here with him.

She'd come down here looking for him for a reason, but now could not recall what that reason was. She wished she had stayed in her—in the bedchamber—he'd loaned her. Then she wouldn't have been privy to his mother's malicious words.

A muscle ticked in Bennett's jaw, a rhythmic reminder of his anger.

She could inquire as to why he was so irritated, but in truth she was afraid to know the answer, afraid that it had something to do with her. "I can't seem to recall why I came down here. Again I apologize for intruding." She turned to go.

"Wait," he said, grabbing her elbow as she passed by him.

"Did you hear something from London? Is Her Majesty well?"

"Yes, no. That is, no I did not hear anything. So as far as I know the Queen is well." He stepped closer to her, so close she could smell the sandalwood in his soap. He waved his hand, an angry slash in the empty space in front of him. Then he swore. Evidently, he'd decided that he no longer felt the need to shield her from such things.

"You and I shall be married," he said.

"I beg your pardon?"

"Your reputation has been compromised. We have no other choice but to marry." His features set in a scowl, he looked at her as if she was a child and he was frustrated at having to explain things to her.

Her heart seemed to stop as if he'd reached into her chest and squeezed it shut. "This is ridiculous. Of course, we are not getting married."

"This is not a discussion," he said. It was as if suddenly the man she'd been with the last two weeks had disappeared and in his place was that stern, rude man she'd once confronted.

"I will not be forced into a marriage with someone who has such little regard for me. Proposals are supposed to, if not contain declarations of love, be flattering and affectionate. You are angry at the thought of having to marry me. No, thank you."

"You think I have no regard for you?" He pulled her

into his arms and kissed her fiercely.

She barely had time to react to the kiss before he ended it, still holding her arms.

"I'll have you know I am very attracted to you and have been since the first moment I saw you."

She recognized he desired her. That much had been abundantly clear every time he pulled her into an embrace. Until last night, she'd thought it was because she favored the queen, but he'd made certain to erase that thought with his murmurs of affection. Still his proposal was horrifically unromantic, not to mention insulting. "Attraction has little to do this."

"Of course it does." His pallor had paled, but anger ticked in the muscles along his jawline. "Why would I marry someone were I not attracted to them?"

She frowned. "So do you want to marry me because of my ruined reputation or because you desire me?"

"What I want has no bearing in this situation. I am honor-bound to marry you."

His words hit as if he'd struck her with his hand. "Yes, just as you were required to work with me on the assignment." She shook her head. "You behave as if you have no choices in your life. The poor, mistreated Earl of Somersby." She blew out a low breath. "As tempting as that proposal is, I'm going to have to decline."

He started to speak, but she put a finger to his lips. "Enough, truly. If you say anything else, I'm not certain I can withstand all the praise and flattery. Suffice it to say, I shall not marry you, nor will I hold you to this. I came to London knowing fully what I was getting into."

She shook her head. "Well, I didn't know everything,

but I decided to continue. And I came to your bed last night knowing what I was doing. If my reputation is ruined, then so be it. I care not a whit what others say in the first place." That wasn't entirely true. She cared what her family thought, and a ruined reputation could damage her younger sisters' chances of marriage. Hopefully though, her elder sisters could more than make up for her slip. She tugged at her sleeves. "Besides, with my sisters around, people don't spend time discussing me. This little rumor, as it were, will disappear in time and people will forget it had ever been said." She turned to leave.

"This is not over," he said.

"Yes, Bennett, it is."

"Where are you going?"

"Back upstairs. I have some thinking to do." Not to mention some writing. Though her own reputation might be damned, she'd just had a brilliant idea for her book.

Chapter Twelve

Bennett knew that Evie was not enthusiastic about their upcoming nuptials; still, they had details they needed to work out together. She had been scarce since his proposal, and he'd tired of waiting for her. So he made his way to her bedchamber to discuss said matters with her.

He was angry, not so much about the forced marriage, but at the rumors that dictated it. Yes, he was the one who had succumbed to her seduction and taken her virtue, but the gossips didn't actually know that. In truth, he was rather relieved about having to marry Evie. He wanted her, but he'd certainly not been willing to pursue her in conventional methods, which is no doubt what she would require for marriage. But now their hands were forced and he'd get the woman he wanted without promises of love and romance.

He knocked lightly, but there was no answer. Perhaps she slept. They'd been up nearly the entire night, and she was no doubt tired. He knocked once more before turning the knob and giving himself entrance.

She was decidedly absent from her room. Not only was she absent, but it would seem that in her very short stay, she'd also taken the liberty to rearrange some of the furniture. Perhaps she had done that to this room when she'd been here the first time. Most notably she had taken the small writing desk and moved it to beneath the window. He walked over to peer outside on the off chance she'd decided to take a walk.

He saw no one out the window, though admittedly several trees blocked his view of the grounds. She could be out there somewhere. His nerves ticked up. After the danger she'd been in, he hated not having her in his sight, but the threat of danger had been removed; she was no longer on the assignment, therefore, he need not be concerned about her safety. Yet, he was, he could not deny that.

"What are you doing in here?" Evie's voice came from behind him.

"I came to appeal to your logical sense."

She crossed her arms over her chest. "There is nothing you can say to convince me to marry you."

"You are ridiculously stubborn." He took a step towards her. "Nothing? Because you don't want to marry me or you don't want to marry at all?"

"I had no intentions of marrying. No man would allow me the freedom to write."

Another step. "Not true. I wouldn't care if you wrote."

Her mouth opened, then she frowned and closed her lips.

"Still unconvinced, I see."

"You don't understand, Bennett." She walked past him

to the window, pulled back the drapery to see down below. "I never wanted to marry, but for one exception."

He'd hoped she wouldn't be so blinded by the foolishness that plagued most women. "You want me to promise to love you forever."

"No. That would be a lie. I don't want you to lie to me."

"That is the most reasonable thing you've said yet." The irony of the situation did not evade him. He'd finally found a woman he would be pleased to marry, yet she was one woman who would say no because he refused her his heart.

She turned around then and faced him. "What did she do to you?"

"What do you think happened between Gwyneth and I? That I walked out on her because I felt like it?"

"I actually have no notion of what happened other than what I've heard from other people," she said.

He never discussed this with anyone. Regardless of the truth, he'd become the villain in everyone's eyes. Normally he did not care what people believed of him, but he found he wasn't willing for Evie to see him in such a way. "I found her in bed. In *my* bed with Morton."

Evie came forward, but made no move to touch him, for which he was thankful.

"She begged me to still marry her despite her indiscretion. When I asked her why..." He shook his head. "My money, she needed my fortune." Then she'd gone on to call him a beast, told him he was abnormal and that no woman would ever truly want him.

"Why did you not defend your name? Tell people the truth?"

"It would not have mattered. People will believe what

they want to believe. With Gwyneth and Morton telling the same story, he came off looking like the hero that swooped in and rescued her poor reputation." She'd cried her pretty tears and Morton had smiled his charming grins and together they'd become the favorite couple that season.

As it turned out, Gwyneth had been right, no woman had wanted him. Perhaps this was Evie's true motivation, but she was too gentle to say as much. What was that old saying? 'Fool me once, shame on you, fool me twice, shame on me.'

• • •

It hadn't been that difficult to sneak away from Bennett's estate, as he'd holed himself up in his study after their argument. Though convincing his staff to assist her in returning home had been more challenging, finally they'd succumbed to her pleading and she'd been in her own bed by a quarter after midnight.

The night had been rough. She kept seeing Bennett's face as he'd told her about discovering Gwyneth with Lord Morton. He must have cared for her dearly to be so convinced that the mere notion of love was a falsehood. She'd cried more than she'd slept, but by the light of the morning sun, she'd decided she had shed far too many tears for Lord Somersby. She'd been a fool to believe a man as powerful and handsome could fall in love with a plain country miss. So after a quick breakfast, she retired to the front parlor to read and enjoy a quiet morning alone.

Mrs. Kimble, the housekeeper, scratched on the door. "Miss Evelyn, there is a gentleman here to see you."

She had wondered if he would come and try to bring her back to his estate, but she had a speech all prepared, a way to release his duty-bound notion of saving her reputation. Then he could go about his business with the Crown. She swung her legs off the arm of the chair and stood, waiting for his broad shoulders and glowering expression to enter the room.

Instead the impossibly handsome Phillip Wells, Earl of Morton stepped inside and bowed slightly. "Miss Evelyn, I'm so pleased to find you well."

"I am admittedly quite surprised by your visit. I had no notion you knew where I lived, Lord Morton." Unease flitted through her, but she swatted it away. This man was harmless, a nuisance, though hadn't Bennett sent one of the other Brotherhood members to discuss some matters with Lord Morton? Had Bennett thought this man part of the assassination attempt? Granted, she knew that Bennett knew the man's character and no doubt thought him capable of any variety of misdeeds.

"I do hope you are not here on official Brotherhood business. Perhaps you were not informed that the Queen has returned and she herself sent me on my way."

He smiled warmly and came forward. "No, I came to see you. I have a business proposal for you." Though she'd only met him one other time, he did appear a little ruffled around the edges today, his clothes not as impeccable, his hair not so perfectly in place. Dark circles weighed heavy under his eyes, indicating he too had spent a sleepless night.

There was a sort of desperate cheerfulness in his smile that she didn't trust. She frowned. "What kind of business could you possibly have with me?"

"Why the same kind of business you had with Bennett of course," Lord Morton said smoothly. For one horrible moment, she thought perhaps he knew the truth about her relationship with Bennett. But then Lord Morton added, "I need you to impersonate our dear monarch one last time."

She frowned. "I'm afraid that I'm retired from my life adventure and am content to stay home with my family."

"Nonsense." He waved a hand, came towards her. "I can assure you that you will not want to miss this particular assignment."

For the briefest second, she considered hearing his proposal. Perhaps more adventure was what she needed. Perhaps that would take her mind off Bennett and the heartbreak he'd caused her. She was tempted for only a moment. In truth, she knew it was a distraction she needed. She needed time to heal her heart, and a more common sense when it came to whom exactly she handed her heart out to. "It is truly kind of you to consider me, but certainly there is someone more qualified than myself."

"On the contrary, you are who I need for this. Come with me, Evelyn." He held his hand out to her.

She shook her head. "No. Thank you." She shook her head, dread tiptoeing up her spine. Suddenly the desperation on his face no longer looked cheerful or charming; that desperation looked dangerous. *He* looked dangerous. I believe I'm going to insist that you take your leave now."

"I'm afraid that's only going to happen if you leave with me," he said.

"Absolutely not!"

He withdrew a pistol from his coat and pointed it straight at her. "Oh, I insist."

• • •

Initially, when Bennett discovered that Evelyn had left his estate, he'd thought to leave her be, go back to London and proceed as if nothing had happened between them, but that thought had been fleeting. Every thought after that had been filled with anger.

He was angry with her for leaving, and he was furious with his staff for allowing her to do so. Nay, for assisting her in doing so. His butler and housekeeper hadn't met his eyes for the last half-hour while they'd readied things for him to leave.

He'd threatened to deal with them when he returned, but it was doubtful he'd do much more than give them a stern lecture on following his orders. He could already hear his housekeeper's explanation, something about how he'd told them that Evelyn was to be their new mistress and following her wishes seemed appropriate.

He was angry with her still, and this little escape of hers hadn't helped cool his ire, but Evie didn't seem to be the sort of woman who would play such games. Doubt nagged at him. Regardless of her motivation, he was coming to get her. Now, as he neared Evelyn's cottage, he considered what he'd say to her. He shouldn't say anything, merely walk in and toss her over his shoulder and bring her back home.

Home.

When had home become where the two of them were? Only since he'd realized he'd have to marry her. This was honor, nothing more.

Evelyn had told him she didn't want to marry, that she

wanted the financial freedom to write her books. That she'd only consider marriage for love. He couldn't offer her that, but he could give her all the freedom she needed for writing and perhaps fatten the dowries for her two younger sisters to ensure they made advantageous matches.

The carriage turned down the drive that led to the Marrington cottage. He hadn't wanted to take a rig, they took longer than being on horseback, but he couldn't expect her to ride behind him all the way back to his estate.

The wheels had barely slowed when he tossed open the door and jumped to the rocky path. He knocked, but didn't have to wait long before the housekeeper opened, a handkerchief blotting her red-rimmed eyes. Her mouth opened, then she started crying again. "Lord Somersby, can I help you?"

He frowned. "I'm here to see Miss Marrington. Miss Evelyn Marrington," he said.

"That's just it, My Lord, she's gone. Missing." She sniffed loudly. "I believe that man took her."

Fear settled like ice in his bones. "Who took her? What man?"

"It's all my fault, I let him in. He said he knew her from London. He seemed so nice, and he was so charming and handsome, with the bluest eyes I've ever seen."

Charming, handsome and with blue eyes, while that might describe plenty of gentlemen in London, Bennett knew of only one who would know of Evie's connection with Her Majesty. Bennett grabbed the woman's arms and made her look at him. "Was his name Lord Morton?"

She sniffed, then nodded. "Yes, I believe it was."

"And Evelyn left with him?"

"I'm not certain how it happened. He came in and by the time I brought them the tea tray, they were gone. Miss Evie simply vanished with him."

Bennett swore. He should have known that Morton would do something foolish. The man could not be trusted. He had given Adrian all the details of Morton's strange behavior, but obviously he hadn't found the man in time. Had Bennett sent the information to Potterfield after the incident in London, or perhaps even after Gwyneth had tried to blackmail him, then perhaps he wouldn't have been a danger to Evelyn. But what the devil would Morton need with her?

Bennett didn't know why Morton had taken her, but none of the reasons he could imagine were good. And his gut told him this was very bad.

· · ·

A quick check of Morton's London townhome revealed neither the Earl nor Lady Morton were home. Not only that, but once pressed, the staff admitted they had seen neither in more than a day, and the last time they'd seen the Earl, he'd been distraught.

Bennett left there feeling a little distraught himself. He had no notion where the man would take Evie, so he did the only thing he could think of and he started at the headquarters of the Brotherhood, the one at the base of Parliament.

It was empty save for a few servants. Next he made his way back to the tunnels beneath Buckingham. Adrian had met him on his way out and explained that he'd also been looking for the man but hadn't seen him.

"Try Hyde Park, you know how Morton loves to be seen," Adrian said. "It is one of his favorite places in town."

"Would he take her to the meeting spot?" Bennett asked.

"He knows about it. I will check back at his townhome and a few clubs and we can meet back here," Adrian said.

Bennett left and headed in the direction of Hyde Park near the old Tyburn Gallows. It was where the Brotherhood did much of their business, close enough to Rotten Row for passersby to assume you were there to enjoy the outdoors, but secluded enough to exchange private information.

Bennett slowed the carriage to a halt two blocks from entrance of the park. He hopped down and snuck quietly through the darkness toward the wooded area. In the distance ripples from the Serpentine lapped softly against the shoreline. The moon hung heavy and low in the sky, lighting his path.

He pulled the pistol out of the back of his pants, then he crept forward. Through the clearing of the trees, he saw Morton standing next to Evie, her petite stature dwarfed by Morton's height. She wore what appeared to be a simple day dress and a cloak, so at least she wouldn't be cold. The riot of curls on her head sprang in every which direction, an indicator of how she'd been treated perhaps. Though her hands were tied, she seemed nonplussed about it.

Bennett stood at the perimeter of the old gallows spot listening. The line of trees hid him well, enabling him to observe. If being a member of the Brotherhood had taught him anything it was to take a moment to assess the situation before he acted. He hadn't always followed this, but Evie's life was at stake and he couldn't afford to be reckless.

"Why are they not here yet?" Morton asked, continually watching the path that led to their hiding place.

"Perhaps you got the location or time wrong," Evie said.

Bennett had to smile. Leave it to her to offer helpful suggestions in the midst of her own kidnapping.

"*I* set this meeting location," Morton said.

While Bennett could see the fear in Evie's tight shoulders, she did her best to put on a brave front. He'd never told her that Morton could be dangerous. He'd allowed his own personal feelings about the bastard cloud his mind and Bennett had missed all the connections. They were here to meet someone, but who would want Evie? Enough of the waiting and wondering, it was time to take action. He certainly wasn't going to stand around and allow that man to hand Evie over to someone more dangerous.

Bennett moved from the line of trees quickly, then stepped out of the shadows, and leveled his gun on Morton. "Hand her over."

Morton started, looked at Bennett, his eyes wide with something far more alarming than fear, the man looked mad. "I can't do that, Somersby." He shook his head and his normally perfect hair swayed with the movement. "They'll kill her."

Bennett frowned, tried to keep his focus on Morton and not look at Evie, not yet. "Who? Who is going to kill who?"

"They have my Gwyneth, they'll kill her."

"Who are they?" Bennett asked.

"These men." He shook his head. "I made a deal with them, I would help them with some tasks and in return they'd pay off my debts. You said it yourself, Somersby, I'm close to being sent to debtor's prison." He winced. "I didn't have any other choice."

Which meant had he given Gwyneth the money she asked for when she'd come to him, then Morton wouldn't have gotten involved with these men and Evie wouldn't be in danger. "What were these tasks?" Bennett asked. He wanted Evie safe, but he also had a responsibility to get some answers to these questions.

"They wanted to know about the tunnels, where they were, how to access them. But I only had a limited amount of information. I came to see where you were keeping her in the palace." Morton said. "They want the Queen. I knew I couldn't get to her, so I brought them the next best thing. They'll never know the difference."

"Who are they?" Bennett asked.

"I don't know. I've never met any of them, only received messages by post and messenger."

Bennett believed him, which meant that continuing to question him would get Bennett nowhere. It was time to remove Evie from this situation. "Evie isn't a part of this, Morton." Bennett took slow steps towards them. "I'll help you save Gwyneth, but first let me get Evie to safety."

"No, I can't." He held the gun up to Evie's head and she released a small shriek. Bennett stopped cold. "Gwyneth is in danger!"

"That's no one's fault but your own." Guilt gnawed at him. Why didn't he just give her money? Bennett took another step forward.

"Bennett, stop. Look at me," Evie said.

He didn't want to look at her. Admittedly he was terrified at the moment, for her, for her safety. Damnation, what had this woman done to him? Gone was all the anger he'd had towards her and in its place was gut-wrenching fear. But he did as she bade, and his eyes locked onto hers. His heart thundered in his chest.

"I understand the dangers of this situation, but if you save me now, we'll never know who they are." She gave him a weak smile; he saw tears swimming in her eyes. "This is bigger than you and me. You must uncover who these people are, who are after Her Majesty."

"I will not risk your life again," Bennett said.

"It is my choice. Allow me to finish this. It might be the only way to catch them," she said. "The only way to keep the queen safe."

"Both of you shut up, I'm trying to think," Morton said. Then he looked at Bennett. "The girl is right. They will believe you're here to deliver the Queen and they'll give me back Gwyneth. Once she's safe, we can capture him, discover who he is working for."

"It's too dangerous," Bennett said.

"I could have already killed her," Morton said plainly.

"And I could kill you," Bennett said.

"Enough from both of you," Evie said. "I believe they're here."

The decision was made for them. Though he worried, Bennett knew Evie was right. If they were to uncover the identity of the people trying to assassinate the queen, he needed to be here for this, play along with the charade. His allegiance should be, first and foremost, to the Brotherhood and the Crown and not Evelyn Marrington. Still, he would never forgive himself if he allowed her to get injured anymore than she already had.

"Morton!" a man's voice called.

"Here. And I have the Queen," Morton said.

The rocks from the path crunched beneath the approaching steps. From where Bennett stood, he could make out two shadows moving toward them, then the pair stopped.

"Who else is with you?" the man yelled.

"Tell him you brought Bennett too," Evie said.

"The Queen's guard dog, I brought you an extra gift," Morton said, not missing a beat. "Put your pistol away, Somersby," he added with a whisper.

Bennett knew what this meant. Morton intended to pass Bennett off as another prisoner, an exchange in addition to the "queen." And all because of Evie's suggestion. What was she thinking?

He pocketed the pistol, but kept his hands in front of him so he could quickly retrieve it if necessary. Morton was behaving more erratic than Bennett had ever seen him. When it came down to it, Bennett wasn't certain he'd be able to reason with the man. And of course he had no idea who this new person was, other than someone who wanted the Queen dead. Bennett kept his hands still and hoped that from a distance it would appear as if his hands were tied as Evie's were.

The man started moving toward them again. "I'll kill her, Morton, you know I will," he called. They came to a part in the path clear enough of the trees for the moon to illuminate them. He had Gwyneth, as Morton had said he did, and she did not appear as if she'd been as well cared for as Evie. Her dress was torn and blood streaked down the left side of her face, matting her hair to her cheek. Bennett suspected the man had struck her there, perhaps with the pistol, to either knock her out or keep her compliant.

"Get on your knees!" the man ordered.

Evie took a step forward. "I will do no such thing. I am your liege!"

"Have you gone mad?" Bennett whispered.

"Trust me." She nodded to him. "On your knees, as the man instructed," she said loudly. Her voice rang with authority. "Both of you!"

Bennett eyed her, mesmerized by her presence. She was magnificent, so brave it was humbling. He wasn't certain that Victoria herself could have handled the situation any better. He fell to his knees, careful to keep his hands pinned in front of him. Morton reluctantly knelt, but kept his pistol out.

"Now, then, you wanted the Queen, you shall deal with the Queen. I am outraged by this entire situation," Evie said.

The man had come close enough that Bennett could see enough of his features. It was the same man who had attacked Evie in her bedchamber—well, in Victoria's bedchamber. He clutched Gwyneth to his grubby side, blood caked on the side of her face and hair, one of her eyes was swollen shut. The man grabbed Gwyneth by the hair and shoved her off into the grass. She fell with a whimper.

"Gwyneth!" Morton yelled, and scurried to be at her side.

The worthless bastard cared not what happened to any of them save her, and Bennett appreciated that the man was out of the way. Now he could control the situation better, if Evie would allow him to do so.

The man walked right up to Evie. He was broad, but not tall, and was barely taller than her. He wore a hat low on his brow. Dirt smudged on the man's cheeks and his clothes strained to cover his muscular form. Bennett tightened his hands into fists to resist the urge to ram his body into the man's.

"Who sent you?" Evie asked.

"No one sent me. I work alone," the man said.

Bennett couldn't help but notice the man spoke with an educated edge to his voice and an authority that was normally reserved for the aristocrats.

"I don't have to answer your questions. You might be queen now, but I don't recognize you as such. Women don't belong on the throne," the man said.

"And you intend to change that, do you?" Evie asked. She was remarkable, Bennett realized, not for the first time. Intelligent and brave, resourceful and creative, she was nothing short of mesmerizing.

As the man got closer to Evie, his meaty fists clenched at his sides, Bennett was primed and ready to attack if the situation called for it, but he would wait and see if Evie couldn't get some information. Trust her, she'd said. He could do that; after all she'd done, he owed her that much.

"If I have to," the man said.

"Killing me won't solve anything," she said.

"I'm not going to kill you. You're coming with me, but we're going to leave the rest of these people behind."

Evie tilted her chin, effectively looking down on the man before her. "I am not intending to go anywhere with you."

"You don't have a choice," the man said. His hand grabbed her arm. Bennett was on him in an instant. He might have been shorter in stature, but the man was strong and Bennett had to work to connect his blows. In the process, he took several himself. Pain shot through his head as one landed square on his jaw. His teeth rattled. The man dropped his gun and Bennett took the opportunity to kick it as hard as he could away from them.

Evie had moved herself steps away from Bennett and the man's scuffle, but it wasn't far enough. He needed to get her out of here. He aimed one blow to the man's face and struck him as hard as he could. While it didn't knock the man unconscious, it did rattle him enough that Bennett was able to stand and grab Evie. He leveled the pistol on the man.

"Get up slowly," he told him. "You are going to give us some bloody answers if I have to squeeze them out of you." Why hadn't he thought to bring restraints? He'd only thought of Evie and getting her to safety. She was certainly impairing his ability to do his job, but wasn't keeping her safe part of his duties?

The man stood, his jaw clinched as if to already refuse answering questions.

"You killed her!" Morton yelled from the ground where he knelt by Gwyneth's body. Then he stood and ran at them, tackling the would-be assassin to the ground again. He put his hands around the man's bulky neck.

"Morton, think of what you're doing," Bennett said. "We need him alive and coherent to answer questions. Our duty is to Her Majesty."

Morton looked up at him, then nodded curtly. He released the man's throat and stood. "I wish I could live with that," he said, then aimed his pistol and shot the man. He fell backwards.

Evie screamed.

"What have you done?" Bennett asked.

"What needed to be done." Morton eyed him. "It matters not, there will always be more. This one was merely one man working for another man."

"What do you know?" Bennett asked.

He shrugged. "I told you. Nothing. I only ever got notes." Then he raised his pistol and pointed it at Bennett and Evie. "Get out of here before I kill the both of you too."

Bennett pulled Evie to him. "We need to get you out of here."

"What about them? We can't leave dead bodies here in the park," she said.

"I shall send for a constable to come and take care of matters, then I'll send a message to the Brotherhood. All will be well." Though he wasn't quite certain he believed that any longer. At least Evie was safe.

"Go!" Morton yelled.

Evie nodded. Bennett noticed the fear lining her eyes and the way she turned her body away from the bleeding man at their feet. With nothing left to say, he grabbed her hand and led her to the carriage. They hadn't caught the assassin, but at least Evie was safe and tonight that was all he cared about.

Chapter Thirteen

Evie wasn't certain her heart would ever slow. The pounding of it seemed to echo through her entire body. She and Bennett didn't speak the entire carriage ride back to her family's cottage. While she missed her family terribly, she was thankful they had yet to return home. She had no interest in sharing the details of the evening with them.

Instead she wanted nothing more than to spend the night in Bennett's arms, desperately trying to forget everything that had happened that evening, though she doubted he'd be agreeable to such a thing, considering.

"I can sleep on the floor in the parlor," he said as they entered the cottage.

She pulled his face down to hers and kissed him fiercely. "No, I want you with me. I need you tonight."

He growled a response, then took her mouth in another kiss. Gone were her fears about whether or not he'd be receptive to her request. In their place was a deep-seeded and simple need to forget anything but the kiss of this man. She wanted to touch him and forget, if only for a moment, all that had occurred tonight.

She broke their kiss long enough to bring him into her bedchamber and close the door behind them. She cared not if the servants knew she'd brought a man into her room, into her bed. The only thing that mattered tonight was this moment with Bennett.

She pressed her lips to his and he took what she gave and demanded more. He pulled her tight to him, kissed her breathless. His fingers made quick work of the buttons on the back of her dress, which soon fell off her body in a pool at her feet. She stepped out of it, then pulled her shift over her head until she stood before him in nothing but her stockings and shoes.

"God, you're beautiful," he said. He tore at his own clothes, removing them quickly.

She too rid herself of the stockings and shoes, and together they lay on her bed. It was much smaller than the grand bed they'd shared at his country estate, but it would suffice.

"Be on top," he said.

She wasn't certain what to do, but in this moment, she would deny him nothing. So she brought one leg across and straddled him. He stopped her before she lowered herself on top of him. Pulled her face down and kissed her again, a long, deep kiss that spoke of things Evie had never dared dream of. Tears pricked at the corners of her eyes, so she kept them closed to keep the tears from falling.

His hand found her; a finger teased her opening. She was already slick with desire for him. Merely the thought of him touching her had lust coursing through her. Now the touch itself was pure pleasure. One finger slipped inside of her while another found her hidden nub. She bucked against him, wanting him to remove his hand so she could slide onto him, but she was spiraling now, the climax hitting hard and fast.

"Now, Evie," he said. He guided her hips, and she lowered herself onto him. He filled her, so full in this position, as if for the first time she could take in all of him.

His eyes latched onto hers and did not look away. She moved, tentative at first, but then she found her rhythm. Over and over again she rocked onto him, keeping her balance by pressing her hands onto his firm chest.

His hand found her again, slid over her sex as she rode him. He was so deep, so full, and with her commanding the pace, she knew when to increase her speed and intensify the force. Deeper and harder she rode him until the world fractured. She shook with her release, but never stopped moving. And then his hit. He grabbed onto her hips, rocking her as a guttural groan escaped from his throat. All the while, he never looked away from her, never closed his eyes.

"Evelyn," he whispered.

The intimacy was so great in that moment that she had to look away for fear he would see into her soul.

• • •

Evie stretched languidly and felt the smile firmly planted on her lips. She and Bennett spent the night making love and holding one another, talking and laughing. It had taken the worst night of her life and ended it with the best night of her life. She had already decided that despite Bennett not loving her, she would rather be with him than without him, regardless of the circumstances. She would accept his proposal and soon she'd be the Lady Somersby.

Eager to tell him, she reached her hand across the bed to touch Bennett, but she found only smooth, cool sheets beneath her fingers. He was gone. She sat upright and searched her small room, a room she had once shared with Jillian.

Voices sounded from beyond her room. Perhaps Bennett had gone to find something to eat. She jumped from the bed to discover she was both delightfully sore from last night's activities and completely naked. Quickly, she donned a shift and dressing gown, then padded her way downstairs.

"Oh, it is so lovely to be home." *Her mother.*

Dear Heaven, had her family returned only to discover her in bed with the Earl of Somersby?

Fear ricocheted through her and she nearly fell down the last few steps. She pulled the dressing gown tighter, then stepped into the parlor. Her mother's favorite room in the house, it was butter yellow from floor to ceiling and housed their nicest furnishings.

"Evie!" Jilly said, jumping to her feet. She ran across the room and flung herself at Evie. They embraced and thankfully Evie's nerves calmed to some degree. She scanned the room, searching for Bennett's handsome face, but saw no sign of him. Her brow furrowed.

"You are finally home," her mother said. "Come, give your mother a hug."

Evie did as she was told and braced herself for the result. What was it about a mother's embrace that could wring out the most stubbornly hidden tears? Her eyes prickled and she squeezed them shut. When he mother released her, she patted Evie's cheek.

"Why the tears, love?" she asked.

Evie shook her head and managed a smile. "I'm just so happy to be home."

Jilly laughed and linked their arms together.

"So where have you been? Truly?" Meghan asked.

Her mother pulled her over to the settee. "Yes, do give us all the details. Your father, well, I'm certain he knows more than he's let on, but he refuses to answer any of my questions."

"Where is Papa?" Evie asked.

"He is resting. Poor dear," Jilly said with a sweet grin. "I'm not certain he thought he'd survive this particular holiday."

"How is your family-to-be?" Evie asked.

"Later," Jilly said. "Right now, we talk about you."

Evie tried to look out the window, but could not see it from where she currently sat. Instead, she saw the eager faces of her family, her delightfully loud family whom she had missed terribly. Bennett was right, they did gossip. Her mother was obnoxious in her quest to marry off her daughters, but they were her family and she loved them.

"You know all those rumors we've heard about Ellis for years?" she said. "Well, as it turns out, they're true."

"What does that have to do with where you were?" Meghan asked.

"I took an assignment with a government organization," she said. "The same agency that Ellis works for."

Her mother's eyes rounded, then her hand flew to her chest. "Good heavens, child, have you lost your senses? Was it dangerous?"

Evie released a sobering breath. "At times, but I was

very well protected." Her heart pinched at the realization that Bennett had deserted her. He'd saved her, yes, and they'd spent a wonderful night together. Still, she'd foolishly hoped that she meant more to him than that. She'd hoped that he'd want more.

"Where were you?" Jilly asked.

"In London. That's really all of the details I can share with you," Evie said. "And you cannot say anything about this to anyone outside of the family."

"Of course not," her mother said. "I admit I was hoping you'd come home from wherever you were married or at the very least betrothed."

"Oh mama, you know that marriage is likely not in my future. But I am happy."

"You can live with me and Eric," Jilly said. She squeezed Evie's hand. "Until you find your love match."

Her sister would never give up that hope for her and Evie was thankful for that, even as she knew it was a futile quest, especially since she had already lost her heart.

Just then the housekeeper stepped inside the parlor. "Luncheon is served."

Evie stood and quickly walked to where Mrs. Kimble stood. Evie put her hand on the older woman's arm. "Mrs. Kimble, did you happen to see a gentleman anywhere in the cottage?"

"No, I didn't. Were you expecting someone?"

"I don't suppose I was. Thank you."

Jilly arrived by her side. "Come, dear sister, come and see my wedding gown."

"We are to eat, Jillian," their mother said.

"It will only take a few moments," Jilly said. She linked

their arms again and led Evie back to the upstairs to their bedchambers. "Who have you been looking for?" Jilly asked once they were enclosed in her bedchamber.

Evie's heart thundered in response. "What are you talking about?"

"You've been searching since you came downstairs. And you asked Mrs. Kimble for someone." Jilly smiled warmly.

Evie thought to evade the question, but decided that would likely get her nowhere. "Lord Somersby brought me home last night." She shook her head. "He must have returned home while I slept. I merely wanted to thank him for his hospitality." That wasn't completely untrue, merely an incomplete truth.

Jilly paused, then nodded. "You know you used to talk to me. We'd stay up late and talk before falling asleep."

Evie smiled. "I remember those nights."

"What changed between us?"

Everything, it seemed. They'd always been close because they were only a year apart. But then Jilly had grown into a poised beauty and Evie had preferred the company of books to balls, and it seemed as if they had nothing in common.

"You know you can trust me with anything. We are family. We always will be and I love you, Evie," Jilly said.

Evie wasn't certain if it was what Jilly said or her nerves being so frazzled after the last several days, but tears stung her eyes. She knew once she began talking, she'd likely not stop. Her mind spun with thoughts and images of Bennett.

"Lord Somersby, I regret to say that I have fallen in love with the man." She ignored the tears and tried to smile. "I know he does not feel the same, and I had told myself that I would be happy, satisfied, with the time we shared together.

But the truth is, I'm not. As it turns out, I want more. A lot more."

Jilly squeezed her hand.

"All these years I told myself that all of the rest of you needed men in your lives to feel complete, but I was different. I didn't need such things, didn't crave them. Instead, I thought that if I only had a bit of funds, I could live alone and write my books and be blissfully happy all on my own."

"But that isn't how you feel?"

"No, not at all. I am such a fool. I suspect I told myself those things in an effort to ignore the fears I had that I would never find a man who wanted me. I'm so very different than you and the rest of our sisters. I am not poised or graceful or lovely."

Jilly chuckled. "No, you are delightfully opinionated, so intelligent it is intimidating, and you've got these lush curves and gorgeous hair. You, sweet Evie, are the Marrington girl who stands out in the crowd."

Evie knew her mouth had fallen open, but she could not hide her surprise.

"We all think so. Meghan is desperately envious of your hair and Portia has always wanted your figure," Jilly said.

How had she gone this long and not known that her sisters thought so differently about herself than she did?

"'Delightfully opinionated,' I suspect mother feels quite different about that than you do."

"Likely true. So Lord Somersby, how do you know he does not feel the same about you?"

There were so many reasons. "He proposed."

"That's wonderful!" Jilly frowned. "Why are you not smiling? The man you love has asked you to marry him."

"He doesn't believe in love," she said. "His life is complicated and dangerous. And I said no."

"But you love him?"

"Desperately."

"Then why would you say no?"

"I wanted him to love me in return." She shrugged. "I am certain my feelings for him will pass with time." She knew that wasn't true, could feel it deep into her soul, but she also knew she'd have to put on a brave face for her sister's sake, and for her mother.

"You don't have to pretend everything is all right. You don't have to put on a brave front," Jilly said.

She had forgotten how perceptive her sister could be. "Yes, I most assuredly do have to be brave. If mother were to suspect how I feel, I would never get a moment's peace."

"You wouldn't get a moments peace. What of poor Lord Somersby? She would likely hunt him down and murder him in his sleep."

They both laughed for a moment. "Trust that I shall endure, Jilly. Lately I have been practicing being aloof. I've gotten quite accomplished at it. And because of my assignment with the agency, I will be compensated handsomely. I should be able to afford a house of my own. Concentrate on my writing, follow through with my original plans."

"But you will be unhappy," Jilly said.

Thankfully she didn't have to reply because Meghan entered the room and informed them that mother insisted they come down for luncheon straight away.

Bennett had left Evie's bed at first light. He'd awoken with the realization that he would never get a good night's rest again if Evie was not his wife. She'd been in danger far too much, and he wanted her with him so he could ensure her safety.

But before he could proceed with their nuptials, he'd had to report everything to the Brotherhood.

"So Morton killed the man?" Potterfield asked.

"Yes. I sent for a constable to deal with the bodies," Bennett said.

"And Morton?"

"Threatened to kill Evie and me. I brought her to safety before I came here." He steeled himself for a lecture from Potterfield on his priorities and how he should have come here first to report on the events of the night. But the man merely nodded.

"Lynford, you go to the park and see if any evidence remains, then go to the morgue to inspect the bodies," Potterfield said.

Lynford stood.

"Glad you've returned, Priest," Bennett said to Lynford.

"I as well. Scotland does not agree with me." Then he faced Potterfield. "I'll report back as soon as I find something."

"Morton is working with someone else. Or several someones. He said they offered to pay his debts if he gave him information."

"So that is how they found the tunnels," Potterfield said.

"Evidently."

"How did he even know about the tunnels?" Ellis asked. "He was not involved in any of that."

"People talk," Potterfield said. "No matter how careful we are, information will get out. I've already placed additional guards in the tunnels for added security." He eyed Bennett for a moment. "You did good work on this one, Somersby."

"Thank you, Sir." He hadn't realized until that moment how much he'd needed that one simple statement. "Is that all?"

"Do you have somewhere else to be?" Potterfield asked.

"I do," Bennett said. He came to his feet.

"Where are you going in such a rush?" Ellis asked.

Bennett grinned. "Epping."

"Developed a fondness for my uncle's sleepy little village, have you?"

"Or a certain woman who lives there."

Ellis nodded. "Hopefully my aunt won't smother you with excitement."

"It's not your aunt I'm worried about. I'm afraid I've been a bit daft when it comes to your cousin and now I must go and do whatever I can to convince her to marry me."

"Be off with you then," Potterfield said. He slid a bag of coin across the table. "Miss Marrington's compensation for her assignment. Do give her my gratitude."

It was getting late in the day, and Bennett was certain he should probably wait for the following morning to see Evelyn, but he'd never been very good at patience. So it was nearing the ten o'clock hour when he knocked on the Marrington cottage door.

The housekeeper answered, her brows rose. "My Lord." She stepped out of his way, giving him entrance. "Come in. They're in the parlor." She opened the parlor door and had announced him before he'd even gotten a chance to request an audience with Evelyn.

He breached the doorway to the parlor and five Marrington women as well as Sir Marrington stood waiting.

"My Lord, what an honor," Mrs. Marrington said.

"I do apologize for the late hour."

"Don't be silly," Mrs. Marrington said. "You are welcome anytime, My Lord."

Evie stood between her sisters; still his wild poppy amidst the field of roses. She was not the same woman he'd taken from this village and brought to London.

All of them watched him expectantly and he wanted nothing more than to be alone with Evie, to merely have a moment to explain to her how he felt. He'd come here, her money from the Brotherhood in his pocket, ready to give her a choice. The future she wanted—freedom to write and live on her own—or perhaps one she hadn't fully considered, one with him.

He glanced at each of their faces. He had not intended to discuss any of this in front of her entire family. Yet, they made no move to leave the room. Her father, at least, had taken a seat, though his newspaper remained on the side table. The women, though, they all looked directly at him, all of them, save Evie.

"Evelyn, could we speak alone?"

One of the sisters grinned widely, but held tightly to Evie's arm. Evie's gaze never wavered, her blue eyes locked onto his. "I believe anything you have to say to me can be said here, within the walls of my family's home. They are well aware of where I've been, though I did not share too many specifics."

She was the most intelligent woman he'd ever known, which meant only one thing—she knew precisely what he intended to say and did not want to hear it. She thought having her family here would prevent him from proposing.

She had made up her mind, it seemed, decided that no

matter what he offered her, she was not interested in being his wife. *No woman would ever want you.*

He reached into his pocket and retrieved the bag of monies owed her. He held it out.

Her brow furrowed, but she took it. The coins jingled as her hand gripped the velvet.

"I believe you'll find this sum more than adequate for your service to the Crown. Her Majesty sends her warmest regards." He bowed slightly.

She took a visibly heavy breath and gave him a curt nod. "Thank you."

He bowed. So this was it. She would no longer be in his life. He tried to grasp the thought, tried to think of something, anything he could say that might change her mind. But ultimately, she had made her choice. She'd told him repeatedly that she had no intention of marrying him. Why should he expect a different answer now?

"My apology to having disturbed your evening." And he turned to go. He'd told Ellis he intended to do whatever he could to convince her to marry him. He hadn't even tried. He hadn't even told her how he truly felt. She might still reject him, confirm Gwyneth's words from so long ago. But damnation, he was going to tell her how it felt. He slowly turned. "No, I can't do this. You might not want to hear what I have to say, but I'm going to say what I've come to say regardless of whether or not you want to hear it."

Her eyes widened, and her lips parted, but she said nothing.

"The truth is, Evie—" He closed the distance between them. "—you are a colossal distraction. You absolutely infuriate me with your headstrong ways, but you're so much more than I could have ever imagined. No one has ever stood up to me the way you do, as if you have no fear. You're more than I ever thought I deserved and you've made me want things I never thought I'd want."

One of her sister's squealed, but he ignored the sound as best he could. Right now he only saw Evie, beautiful, infuriating Evie who had irrevocably stolen his heart. He loved her. Wholeheartedly and unabashedly loved her.

"I know that my life isn't simple, but if you can fool all of London into thinking you're the Queen, then I think you're up for the task."

Her mother gasped.

Still the frown remained on Evie's expression. "What are you saying, Bennett?"

"For being so bloody smart, you are daft sometimes." He pulled her to him, not caring about the impropriety of the embrace. "I'm saying that I love you. Desperately. Despite the fact that you are maddening, I love you and I want to marry you."

All of her sisters screamed and her mother called for the smelling salts.

And Evie, she laughed amidst a few stray tears, then she flung herself into his arms. "It's about time you figured this out."

"I'm an idiot." He smothered her head in kisses. "Please say you'll marry me."

"Yes, a thousand times, yes!"

And he pulled her into his arms for a none-too-proper kiss.

OTHER BOOKS BY ROBYN DEHART

About the Author

National bestselling author Robyn DeHart's novels have appeared in the top bestselling romance and historical romance lists. Her books have been translated into nearly a dozen languages. Her historical romantic adventure series, The Legend Hunters, were not only bestsellers, but also award winners, snagging a Reader's Crown and a Reviewer's Choice award. She'll have four releases in 2014 and already has three on the calendar for 2015, all set in the popular historical romance Regency and Victorian eras.

Known for her "strong dialogue and characters that leap off the page" (*RT Bookclub*) and her "sizzling romance" (*Publishers Weekly*), her books have been featured in *USA Today* and the *Chicago Tribune*. A popular writing instructor, she has given speeches at writing conferences in Los Angeles, Washington DC, New York, Dallas, Nashville, and Toronto, among many others.

When not writing, you can find Robyn hanging out with

her family, husband (The Professor) a university professor of political science, and their two ridiculously beautiful and smart daughters, Busybee and Babybee, as well as two spoiled-rotten cats. They live in the hill country of Texas where it's hot eight months of the year, but those big blue skies make it worth it.

Made in the USA
Charleston, SC
17 September 2016